"If you need me, I'm here," Leo said softly

Taking a deep, unsteady breath, Corinne stepped back. As much as she wanted Leo, she had to keep her secret. Just a little longer.... "I'm okay," she lied. Backing away from the door, she murmured, "It's getting late."

Leo searched her face as though trying to gauge her mood. "You're right," he said finally. "I should go." Then his green-eyed gaze dropped and a corner of his mouth kicked up in a lopsided grin. "What's that on your shirt?"

She looked down. Oh-oh.... She looked at her nightshirt, suddenly noticing the words written on the front—*I'm Not Sleepy, Are You?*

Leo's grin settled into an intimate smile. And in that instant, Corinne remembered what it had been like when his lips had taken hers. Hot. Ferocious. And when his hands—roughened and strong—had caressed her. She opened her mouth to speak, but her voice refused to work. It didn't help that Leo was staring at the words emblazoned on the part of the shirt that covered her breasts. "It's—I'm—"

"It's okay," he said, moving closer. "I'm not sleepy, either...."

Dear Reader,

Have you ever wanted to run away from it all—
maybe in a splashy, to-die-for car to boot—and
become someone else for a few days? Someone who's
wildly, provocatively different? In a place where you
could act out a lifestyle you've always dreamed about?

Well, Corinne McCourt, my heroine, gets that
chance...although she really didn't *mean* to steal
her ex-fiancé's Ferrari, exchange her boring skirts
and blouses for slinky dresses or end up taking the
job of a bikini-clad babe in a Las Vegas boxing ring!
But for all the external changes in her life, perhaps the
most profound change is in the person she becomes....

And of course, it doesn't hurt that a detective who has
the charm of Mel Gibson and the attitude of Billy Idol
enters her life, curious to figure out just what kind of
woman Corinne's pretending to be—and liking what
he finds....

So enjoy the ride—the *Joyride*, that is—and indulge in
a few fantasies of your own.

Colleen Collins

Books by Colleen Collins

HARLEQUIN DUETS
10—MARRIED AFTER BREAKFAST
22—ROUGH AND RUGGED
30—IN BED WITH THE PIRATE
39—SHE'S GOT MAIL!

Don't miss any of our special offers. Write to us at the
following address for information on our newest releases.

Harlequin Reader Service
U.S.: 3010 Walden Ave., P.O. Box 1325, Buffalo, NY 14269
Canadian: P.O. Box 609, Fort Erie, Ont. L2A 5X3

JOYRIDE
Colleen Collins

HARLEQUIN®

TORONTO • NEW YORK • LONDON
AMSTERDAM • PARIS • SYDNEY • HAMBURG
STOCKHOLM • ATHENS • TOKYO • MILAN • MADRID
PRAGUE • WARSAW • BUDAPEST • AUCKLAND

To my editor, Brenda Chin, for keeping the faith.

ISBN 0-373-25967-0

JOYRIDE

Visit us at www.eHarlequin.com

Printed in U.S.A.

CORINNE MCCOURT STOOD in front of the full-length mirror and checked out her naked twenty-eight-year-old body. At five-six—give or take a few inches—she wasn't exactly statuesque, but had strong legs thanks to her morning runs and a compact behind thanks to genetics. She looked at her rounded breasts and wished her live-in fiancé Tony Borgeson felt thankful for them again. Once upon a time he'd called them his "luscious vanilla double scoops." She tilted her head. "They still look scoopable," she whispered, hating the question in her voice. What happened? Five years ago, when they first got involved, he couldn't scoop enough. She'd nicknamed him Bulldozer.

These days she was lucky if she got even a little dozer.

Playing with the gold heart pendant around her neck, Corinne surveyed the full-length mirror she'd installed a month ago—one of her recent ploys to put some va-va-voom back into their relationship. She'd read in a women's magazine where couples and mirrors could be a lethal libido combo that ignited the fires of love.

Unfortunately, the only thing mirrors ignited in Tony was admiration for himself. Every morning, he preened in front of that mirror more than a pet parakeet she'd had as a kid, checking out everything from his stylish tie to his killer smile. She once reminded him that he sold *computers*. Who cared about his smile? Never breaking eye contact with his reflection, he'd announced that a sale was a sale—whether it was lawn mowers or laptops—and first impressions were everything.

She looked down at her very *unimpressive* tummy. To think most women complained their stomachs weren't flat enough! Not Corinne. What she'd give to have a round tummy. Round and full with child. Growing up as an only child, Corinne had dreamed of having a large family of her own. A family who stayed put, like Tony's large Italian family who'd lived in this section of Denver for generations. Unlike Corinne, who—due to her mother's various marriages and near-marriages—had moved six times by the time she was nineteen.

She slid her fingers over her midriff, remembering her girlfriend Cheryl, when she'd been eight months pregnant, saying her baby was crowding her heart. "I want my heart crowded, too," Corinne pleaded softly. Which meant she had to pin the wedding date—something Tony swore he wanted to do but never got around to—and rev his engine just the way he revved his precious Ferrari, which he'd nicknamed "Baby."

His choice of a nickname had always confused Corinne—didn't he realize how much she wanted a baby? *Their* baby? But remembering her mother's words ("If you want a man to do something, honey, show 'im. Don't tell 'im."), Corinne had kept her mouth shut. She'd never been as flamboyant as her mother, so showing wasn't easy for Corinne. But today, despite her flutterings of anxiety—mixed with excitement—

Corinne was going to show, *really* show, the things she wanted. Passion. Intimate communion with her hubby-to-be. And, eventually, there'd be...

"...A new baby," Corinne murmured. Yessiree, with her new va-va-voom plan, she'd be married and pregnant before Tony ran out of killer smiles.

To get things va-vooming, her best pal Kyle had suggested she borrow his book *How to Make Your Man Howl.* Playing by the book, following all the rules, were right up Corinne's alley...but the sizzlingly sexy ideas in *How to Make Your Man Howl* nearly curled Corinne's already wavy hair. Okay, previously she'd attempted some sizzle by hanging the bedroom mirror, but that act had challenged every cell in her inhibited body. She'd been so anxious nailing the mirror to the wall, the darn thing hung at an angle. And her desired result had backfired. Tony, preoccupied with the angle instead of the ardor, instructed her to next time hire a carpenter.

After the mirror idea cracked, Kyle reminded her that *How to Make Your Man Howl* had worked wonders in his relationship with Geoff. And if a gay man didn't understand what made men tick, who did?

So Corinne had flipped through some of its chapters: "Handcuffs Aren't Just for Criminals," "Getting Wild in the Outdoors," "Be a Gift—Let Him Unwrap You." Corinne wasn't sure about the handcuffs. They didn't look very sexy in cop flicks. And outdoors? Her neighbor, old Mr. Valdez, might have a coronary. But being unwrapped? Heck, everybody in the world undressed every day...according to the book, all she had to do was think sexy in the process.

So she planned the grand unveiling for today. Normally, every June 8, she attended her company's annual picnic. Corinne had been at Universal Shower Door almost as long as she'd been with Tony—five years, give or take a month. And every annual picnic she showed up with her annual dish, Jell-O Surprise.

But not this year.

This year she was going to serve *Corinne Surprise* when Tony came home for lunch. A hot thrill zigzagged through her as she imagined his look of shock, then hot arousal, when he found his fiancée, the gift!

Corinne glanced at the clock on the nightstand. Eleven-ten. Tony would be home in twenty minutes. Gift-wrapping time! She grabbed the cylinder of clear plastic wrap she'd purchased this morning at the supermarket. With trembling fingers, she began crookedly wrapping the slick material around her. Well, so what if it wasn't on straight. Unlike the mirror, this plastic stuff wasn't meant to stay on long. *Minutes,* tops.

Humming one of her favorite Céline Dion tunes, Corinne checked her progress in the mirror. She imagined her sleek lines as the lines of his precious Ferrari—the glossy, shimmering coating like the slick, soapy water that sluiced over the car's body when he washed it. Except, unlike with his Ferrari, Tony would lose control with Corinne and tear off the plastic. And amid the ripping, groaning and howling, she'd tease him to take extra care with her bumpers.

Me, teasing like that? She pressed a fingertip against her bottom lip, as though pushing back the forbidden thought. Then she dropped her hand and giggled softly. "I've installed a mirror, dressed hot in freezer wrap. Maybe the new Corinne sometimes jokes during lovemaking, too!" She was liking this new side of herself. Maybe, after the let-'er-rip sex, she'd even be bold enough to demand they set a wedding date. After all, Tony's large Italian family expected it, so with a little sizzling encouragement, Corinne would help nail that expectation. Gee, considering she was on the brink of nailing a date, what should she ask for? Five months from now? Five weeks?

She checked the clock. Five minutes to show time! She finished wrapping herself, then reached for her sewing basket to retrieve a pair of scissors. As she fumbled through spools, fabrics and buttons, it struck her as funny how, after years of sewing practical skirts and demure blouses, here she was snipping off the end of a clear plastic minidress that showed *way* more than her intentions!

After cutting a slit so she could walk, Corinne turned to the mirror and checked out the overall effect. "They wouldn't call me Inconspicuous Corinne at work now!" Her breasts swelled over the minidress like two luscious scoops. Her perky nipples pressed through the clear sheath. And below, through layers of shimmering plastic, you could see a curly triangle. She gave her head a toss, liking the tousled effect of her newly colored shoulder-length glossy blond hair. Wilder, more daring than her normal red hair, which was turning a sedate auburn. Plus this new, sassy blond was almost the same color as Tony's Ferrari— that rare "hot gold" he bragged about to his pals.

"Now for the pièce de résistance," she gloated, tiptoeing to the closet. She'd bought a pair of black stiletto heels especially for this occasion. On her allowance, she'd have had to save for *weeks* to buy these shoes. But Lady Luck had been on her side—they'd been half price. When the middle-aged salesman said their price was slashed because women never wore heels like this anymore, she'd felt her face burn hot, certain he knew she was buying them for sex. When he'd asked her to walk in them, she'd stumbled a few feet, stopped, and swaying a little had squeaked, "They're perfect!"

Okay, it was going to be a challenge walking in these skyscrapers again, but she was a woman on a mission. A make-love-to-her-fiancé mission. A get-married mission.

A make-a-baby mission.

Slipping into the high heels was tougher than she remembered back at the shoe store. The arch was so high, she had to shove her foot in. Reminded her of the time she'd shoved her wild cousin Sandee through the back window of some guy's Chevy. That had been fifteen years ago when Corinne and her mom moved to a small Texas town, following her mom's divorce number two, to be close to the only family Corinne had ever known—Aunt Judy, her mom's identical twin, and Judy's daughter, Sandee. Since those teenage years, Corinne rarely saw Sandee, who now lived in Las Vegas, although they had occasional phone calls where they girl-talked for hours. One of those calls had been just last week...Sandee had been worried about a *bump and run*, but didn't give details. And Corinne didn't pry, although she'd been dying to ask questions because Sandee's *bump and run* sounded like a possible chapter in *How to Make Your Man Howl*.

"Eiiyyy!" Corinne emitted her own howl as she teetered in the heels. Stumbling a few feet, she grabbed the mahogany bedpost and caught her balance. Holding on to the smooth wooden pole, she sucked in several shaky breaths. *This is crazy. I won't look like a hot babe if I'm teetering and stumbling, flailing my arms for balance.* For a stinging moment, she thought she was going to cry.

No! She pressed her lips together, careful to not smudge her lipstick. I *want* to be married. I *want* a baby. I'm going to be sexy if it kills me! Realizing her last thought, she started giggling uncontrollably. "I look like a walking—well, stumbling—ad for *How to Make Your Man Howl*," she whispered to herself. "If this kills me, at least I'll go out of this world looking like one burning hunkess of love! Talk about 'showing'!"

Grinning with a surge of confidence, she straightened, let go of the bedpost, and teetered toward the foyer.

Scratch. Click.

Tony's key in the lock!

Corinne almost tripped as she skidded to a stop in front of the door. Show time! She stood, spread-eagled. What to do with her hands? She flashed on the chapter "Bondage—It's Not Just for Breakfast Anymore." Shakily, she held her hands above her head, wrists crossed.

The door creaked open. Corinne closed her eyes and breathed in deeply, forcing her double scoops high. She felt like an overheated car engine, ready to rip loose and roar...

"Stop it!" squealed a nasally woman's voice. "Wait'll we get inside, Tiger Boy."

Tiger Boy? Corinne opened her eyes. Some frizzy-haired blonde, her body squeezed like a sausage into a low-cut pink number, was nuzzling and rubbing against...Tony!

He looked up, his dark eyes meeting Corinne's. His killer smile died. "This isn't want you think," he said sharply, gesturing emphatically with the hand that wasn't around the blonde.

Corinne's insides shattered, like a splintered mirror. *Think?* She couldn't even breathe. Hell, she couldn't even move! Feeling ridiculously vulnerable, she wanted to cover her nearly naked body but her hands felt soldered to the top of her hot-gold head.

The blonde reared back. "What the hell—?" She turned to Tony. "Is that your cleaning lady?"

"Cleaning—?" A burning rage tore through Corinne, thawing her frozen state. Dropping her hands, she fisted them in front of her. She'd never hit anyone or anything in her life—but right now she could probably cream Mike Tyson. "That's right! I'm the cleaning lady, the seamstress, the washer woman...everything but the banker because ol' Tiger Boy here takes my checks and only gives me a frickin' allowance."

She'd never seen that look on Tony's face. Slack jawed. His eyes wide, dark. For a hotheaded Italian, he was suddenly acting very, very cool. No, make that shocked. And not at her gift-wrapped getup, but at her reaction. Corinne had *never* yelled at him. *Never* spoken her mind. Well, she'd only just started!

As she stepped from one high-heeled foot to the other, like a runner prancing before a race, a drop of sweat rolled down her chest and disappeared between her plastic-wrapped scoops. In the back of her mind, it hit her that suddenly she wasn't teetering.

"To sum it up," she continued, not caring that she was yelling, "I'm the wife-who-wasn't!" She fought the urge to cry and scream as she finished. "And obviously, I'm also the last one to know!"

"Tony," whispered the blonde, "I think your cleaning lady is helping herself to the liquor cabinet—"

Tony cut her off. "Baby," he said, tossing his keys on a side table. "Why don't you go into the other room..."

Baby. Corinne could almost forgive the nickname for his car—but for another woman? While his fiancée was so desperate to get married and have a baby?

"Don't tell *me* to calm down!" The blonde jabbed his chest with an inch-long crimson nail. "You bring me to your house for a nooner and we're greeted by some plastic-wrapped maid with a deranged wife fantasy?"

Corinne's heart twisted. *Plastic-wrapped. Like leftovers.* But the blonde had one thing right. Corinne definitely had a deranged wife fantasy. She'd been a fool wanting to marry this two-timing, self-absorbed Tiger Boy...who had a lot of nerve wearing that crucifix his mother had given him, as though *he* needed protection from the evil in the world!

Corinne glanced at his car keys on the table. Tony and the blonde were yelling at each other as though Corinne didn't exist. Here she was, dressed like some kind of hausfrau hooker, and she was *still* being treated like Inconspicuous Corinne.

Well, no more!

Minutes ago, she'd shakily wrapped herself in this getup, thrilled at her audacious first step at shedding her inhibitions. Well, forget first steps. She was taking a flying leap!

In a rush of movement, Corinne snatched the keys off the table. In a stiff-kneed speed walk, she beelined past the arguing couple and across the lawn to the Ferrari parked in the driveway. Jumping inside, she shoved the key into the ignition. As the engine roared to life, Tony tore across the lawn, yelling a string of profanities—some Italian, some English.

Corinne didn't try to decipher which was which as she shoved the gear into reverse and squealed down the driveway, smoking rubber obliterating the vision of her home, her husband-to-be, her future. In a moment of dread, mixed with a strange anticipation, she realized she was shedding more than her inhibitions, she was shedding her entire life.

As she ground the gear into first, she stuck her other hand out the sunroof. "Bye bye, Baby!" she yelled before punching the gas.

A MANILLA FOLDER LANDED with a slap on Leo's desk. "Guy claims an oversized redhead stole his classic Studebaker," said a gravelly male voice. "More like a classic bump and run. Couldn't have been Lizzie 'cause she had a thing for Acura Integras."

Leo slugged a mouthful of scalding coffee. Too hot. But damn if he'd let on he'd just singed a layer of skin off his tongue.

"Sorry," Dom murmured, rubbing his temple. "Shouldn't make Lizzie jokes. Bad taste."

Real bad. Leo coughed and stared at the folder, pretending to be absorbed in this Studebaker case, but his mind was on Elizabeth—Lizzie—his former wife. Everybody had known how much he loved her. Hell, everyone loved her. She'd had a knack for getting to people with her infectious devil-may-care style.

And just as everyone had known Lizzie, everyone knew the story. How he'd been on a raid and discovered his devil-may-care wife was no angel. Caught her in a drug-bust sting. How he'd been shot at damn near point blank range because he'd been tunnel-visioned on his wife, unable to move, to digest the hellish reality. After getting out of the hospital, the department had pressured him to see a shrink but it had ripped his gut apart to talk about her, so he'd stopped going. Since then, he never talked about her to anyone else. Except Mel, the parrot, and then only after a few drinks.

But even then, he never called her "Lizzie." Always "Elizabeth" as though saying her full, Christian name could distance the devil.

"When do I get a *real* case, Dom?" asked Leo, changing the subject. "I'm thirty-five, your best detective, and you're assigning me senior citizen nits. Next I'll be tracking a stolen walker." But in Leo's heart, he wondered if he even wanted a "real" case. He figured he kept asking because being a cop was the only job he'd ever known.

Dom lifted his eyebrows, which lay like a fuzzy caterpillar across the captain's brow. He opened his mouth to respond, but Leo cut in.

"If you'd gotten shot because your wife was..." The rest of the sentence tasted bitter, so Leo let it hang. *Defensive. Again.* One of his newer, more pleasant personality traits since the crash-and-burn of his marriage, his life. "Forget it." He picked up a pen. "Studebaker," he repeated, writing the word on a legal pad. "Overage geriatric owner. Oversized—whatever that means—redheaded thief." He stopped writing and looked up. "And who said Vegas has become nothing but a big family town?"

Leo had lived here all his life. Watched his dad walk out on the family. Watched his mom raise her two sons single-handedly, one of whom was hell on wheels. By seventeen, Leo had been an accomplished delinquent who specialized in hot-wiring cars for joyrides...but his hobby came to a screeching halt when his mom remarried, this time to a cop.

At first Leo hated his new stepfather, whom Leo called "Hobo Cop" behind his back. But despite Leo's attitude, his stepdad never wavered on dishing out discipline...or love. One day, Leo accidentally called this man "Dad." And when the man, in return, called him "Son," Leo knew he wanted to grow up to be a cop.

Which he became. And after that, a hotshot detective. But now he was on desk duty, his career stalled. Just like his life. Some days he wanted to start over, pack up his antiquated Airstream and head out to some new frontier, finding a small ranch in which to spend the rest of his days. Especially while recovering from the shooting, he'd had a lot of time to indulge in this fantasy. In his darker moments, it'd given him hope to plan how long it'd take to save for a down payment on this ranch...he'd figured two years would nail it...

The sound of Dom shoving aside a bag of pretzels and a half-eaten Twinkie brought Leo back from the ranch fantasy to the desk reality. "You should eat better," Dom grumbled, planting himself on the edge of the desk. Crossing his arms over his uniformed chest, Dom continued, "I know you hate desk duty. Trust me, if we had our way in the precinct, we'd pay you to stay home." Dom grinned, then turned somber again. "It's tough enough getting shot—worse being forced to take a paid leave. Let me remind you that you were to remain on leave for a full year, but not Leo Wolfman—"

"I would've had to take my parrot to AA if I stayed home one day longer."

Dom cocked his eyebrow, which looked as though the caterpillar was arching its back. "He wouldn't drink wine if you didn't pour him a glass."

"Hate to drink alone. Besides, Mel gets cranky when he's sober."

"A parrot named after Mel Gibson," Dom muttered, shaking his head.

"My alter ego. He gets to see real action in those cop flicks with Danny what's-his-name. Not sit behind some desk playing male secretary."

"You're not a secretary, you're a detective."

Leo did a dramatic double take. "And these four months I've been fetching coffee and typing with two fingers, dreaming one day I'd be promoted to office manager."

Dom heaved a sigh. "Why don't you stay home and let Mel do desk duty? At least he doesn't talk back...too much."

Leo had bought the parrot after Elizabeth took the furniture, Acura, even his hallowed collection of Hot Wheels while Leo was in the hospital recuperating. He hadn't really cared that she cleaned out the place—saved him dumping anything that reminded him of her. But when the hospital released him to go home, it had been lonely.

Damn lonely.

That's when he'd decided to buy a pet. One that wouldn't be underfoot all the time. A parrot seemed perfect. A flying, lighthearted, conversational pet. Unfortunately, Mel preferred to walk, had the attitude of a curmudgeon, and wouldn't talk unless he felt like griping. The two of them housebound was like a bad remake of *Grumpy Old Men*.

Old men. Leo glared at the folder. "I didn't become a detective to follow up on old lady purse snatchers and old men car nabbers."

"Give me a break, Wolfman. You've been through a trauma—the department's easing you in. Think of this as a promotion. You're graduating from purses to Studebakers."

Dom had a point. But Leo wouldn't give him the satisfaction of admitting as much. "When I wrap up this Studebaker mystery, give me something I can sink my teeth into."

Dom squinted at Leo, as though to see him better. After a pause, he stood up and brushed some pretzel crumbs off his pants. "Wrap this one up nice and neat, and we'll talk."

Dom's word was better than a signature. "We'll talk" meant Leo had a chance to break out of desk hell. "Deal."

CORINNE STOOD ON the porch of her best buddy Kyle's apartment and jabbed at the doorbell. She prayed he'd answer the door—she wasn't in the mood to flash his partner, Geoff, who despised her. Kyle had once explained that Geoff got jealous of the time Kyle and Corinne spent together—that Geoff viewed Corinne as "the other woman."

"Me, the other woman," she muttered, holding one hand over her breasts, the other over her thighs, not sure if she was really covering anything at all. "I can't excite my fiancé, but a gay man views me as competition."

The door swung open. Kyle, a chocolate-dipped strawberry in his hand, leaned over a little, a look of shock on his face. "Corinne?" His gaze wandered down her plastic-wrapped torso. "What are you doing dressed in company property?"

They both worked at Universal Shower Door, which had a sideline of shower curtains as well. "Like it?" she asked in a high-pitched squeal that bordered on hysteria. "I'm also wearing curtain rings as earrings!"

Kyle gently pulled her inside. "Honey, honey, honey," he murmured, holding her close.

That did it. She'd been strong facing Tony's infidelity. And nothing short of courageous driving across Denver in a see-through getup while madly pumping pedals in stilettos. But right now, she was tired of being strong. Sinking against Kyle, she sputtered tearfully, "Tony. Gift-wrapped. Blonde."

Kyle paused, then said quietly, "If Tony has a thing for gift-wrapping blondes, he should be ecstatic that his fiancée now has beautiful golden locks..." He stepped back and looked into her eyes. "What happened, honey?"

She swallowed, hard. "I took your advice and made my man howl, all right—I stole his macho sports car."

"You *stole* Baby Ferrari?"

"Yes, stole," she admitted, "and I'm never returning *it* or *me* to him. From now on, I'm my own woman." She hadn't even known she felt that way until she'd blurted the words. It was as though her shattered insides were resolidifying into a new Corinne. But her bravado shrank a little. A new Corinne with no home. No money. No clothes. "I'd ask to stay here, but Geoff would freak—"

"To put it mildly."

"I'm in a bind."

Kyle looked her up and down. "To put it strongly." He dangled the strawberry between them. "Want a bite? Sweets for the..." He looked her up and down. "...spicy?"

"No thanks." She grinned. Only Kyle could make her laugh in the middle of a life crisis. Gesturing toward the road, she said, "I can't park that Ferrari on a public street—when Tony figures out I'm not returning, he'll call the police, and they'll find it faster than Geoff can say 'the other woman.'" She sucked in a ragged breath. "Tony's been fooling around on me. With a dumpy blonde with the most *non*luscious vanilla scoops you've ever seen!" The image of that overpacked blonde hurt. Deep.

Kyle waited a moment before responding. "Dumpy?" He snorted dramatically. "He should be jailed! As for those nonvanilla scoops—"

"Non*luscious*—"

"We should sic the Baskin and Robbins police on him!"

"And tell them to stick him in a freezer, dressed only in a pair of his tiger-striped G-strings." No doubt that's where Blondie got "Tiger Boy." Corinne was tempted to add a few more imaginative punishments for Tony when she heard a noise inside the apartment. "Who's here?"

"Geoff and a few friends."

"What're they doing here?"

"Well, Geoff lives here. The others are a few out-of-town friends who're spending the week with us."

"Oh God." Teetering a little on her high heels, Corinne grabbed Kyle's arms for balance. "What am I going to do? It's bad enough I've stolen Tony's Ferrari. Now I'm naked in an apartment filled with strange men."

Kyle chuckled. "All men are strange, darling, but these happen to also be *gay*. So trust me—you're safer than a meatball at a vegetarian banquet." He nibbled on the end of the strawberry while looking her over. "We need to get you into clothes—" He met her eyes. "—then plan what's next in the life of Corinne McCourt."

Kyle offered her his arm. "As we have to pass through the dining room to get to the bedroom where we can raid Geoff's closet, I suggest we pretend you're Judy Garland and I'm Fred Astaire strolling along in the *Easter Parade*."

"Was Judy naked?"

"Yes, but she wore a hat."

"You're lying." She took Kyle's arm. "This isn't fair. You're fully dressed. I'm almost nude."

Kyle shot her a whimsical smile. "Trust me, darling, no one will notice."

2

AN HOUR LATER, Corinne headed west along I-70, tearing across the blacktop in a low-cut slinky number, looking like a Liza Minelli wanna-be from her *Cabaret* days. Piled on the back seat were a stack of Geoff's dresses—a variety of skimpy, sequined numbers that Cher would kill for. Geoff had gone full-tilt drama queen upon hearing Kyle and Corinne would be raiding Geoff's closet. But when Kyle mentioned Corinne would be forced to live with them until she rebuilt her wardrobe, Geoff became ultra magnanimous, offering her dresses, makeup, even a rhinestone dog collar that doubled as a tiara.

She took it all. Anything was better than a roll of plastic wrap.

Then she, Kyle, and four gay men brainstormed her next steps. Everyone agreed she needed an R and R—a fun, relaxing, adventurous getaway before making any serious life changes.

"You never play!" Kyle had chided. "And, darling, you deserve some *major* playground time after what Tigger's put you through." After she told them about "Tiger Boy," they'd coined a new nickname, Tigger, to take some of the sting out of the situation. It sort of worked. The way a salve momentarily takes the sting out of a scraped knee.

Or a joke momentarily takes the sting out of a broken heart.

Determined to mend that broken heart, Corinne mulled over Kyle's comment about "playground time." It took her all of two seconds to associate that concept with her cousin Sandee. Wild, fun-loving Sandee—the complete opposite of mild, sedate Corinne. Maybe, on the outside, they were as different as oil and water, but mix them up, and some secret part merged, forming a special world only they shared. A world where they let down their guards and discussed their dreams and fears...a world where they discovered that, deep inside, they weren't so different after all.

Fortunately, Universal Shower Door owed Corinne several weeks' vacation. As the guys cheered her on, Corinne phoned her cousin in Vegas who, after hearing about Tony's two-timing, had demanded Corinne "get her butt out here, *now.*"

Kyle's friends then took up a collection. After a group hug, where Corinne confessed with a giggle that she'd always wanted to be held by four men at once, she was now driving a stolen Ferrari across the country with three hundred and fifty dollars in her new silver-beaded purse.

It was like being a glamorous Louise minus the Thelma.

Two days later, Corinne arrived on Sandee's doorstep. After squeals of reunion and multiple hugs, Sandee pulled Corinne inside the pink-and-orange living room that made her feel as though she'd stepped into a sunset.

Or, considering she was restarting her life, a sunrise.

Sandee stuck a cigarette between her glossy peach lips and fired the tobacco with the snap of a silver lighter. After exhaling a stream of blue smoke, she smiled—an expression that had always looked more secretive than happy on Sandee. "We still look alike," she said in her signature husky voice.

Their mothers had been identical twins, so Corinne and Sandee did look eerily alike, but their outward personalities were about as similar as Angelina Jolie and Gwyneth Paltrow.

Sandee planted her hands on her curvaceous hips, barely covered in a pair of denim shorts, and gave Corinne a once-over. "And we're still the same size."

Corinne darted a glance at Sandee's breasts. "Well, give or take a few cups."

Sandee waved her frosted-pink fingernails, tipped with tiny red roses, in a dismissive motion. "Honey, inserts can turn Bs into Ds." She narrowed her eyes and scrutinized Corinne's hair. "What's with the bottle blond?"

"It's hot gold. I colored it—" She bit her lip, hating to confess the truth, but knowing Sandee was the one person to whom she could. Corinne took a fortifying breath. "I colored it to remind Tony of his beloved Ferrari," she finished quickly.

Sandee took a long drag on her cigarette, her eyes shooting fire, like the color of her hair. "That bast—" She released the rest of the word on a burst of smoke. She took a few steps, pivoted, and jabbed her cigarette at the air as she spoke. "Honey, *never* change yourself for a man. Never, never, never. Been there, done that."

Sandee's blue eyes softened with a look that gave away that "been there, done that" hadn't been so long ago. "If you feel an overwhelming urge to change something, honey, change it for *you*." She shrugged apologetically. "Uh, sorry I cussed."

"Cuss away," murmured Corinne, but her thoughts were on the other things her cousin had said. Tough, strong Sandee changed herself for a guy? He must have been a very special man to have pierced her tough-skinned "been there, done that" exterior. From the pained expression in Sandee's eyes, Corinne guessed her cousin had been pierced all the way to her heart. But even if that were true, Corinne knew Sandee would never let the world know.

"Cuss away," Corinne repeated, realizing she'd been staring intently at her cousin, but not wanting to voice what she'd been thinking. "You can call Tony whatever you like. Except Tiger Boy." Corinne grinned, feeling silly and happy that she could play with that term.

"You got it." Sandee smiled, that sly, secretive smile that reminded Corinne of the Cheshire Cat. "No T. Boy. Besides, I have a list of *much* better names for that bozo after what he did to you. But I'll not use them all at once—I'll sprinkle 'em like salt on food...just enough to spice up our conversations." She pointed at Corinne's high heels. "Speaking of spice, dig the stilettos." Her blue-eyed gaze roamed up the silvery body-hugging dress. "Cool look, too. Looks good with that heart necklace Aunt Charlene gave you."

Corinne's fingers touched the locket, the sole item from her former life. A gift from her mom on Corinne's sixteenth birthday. A flickering of sadness rose within her as she realized she'd done exactly what her mother had done so many times—run away from a man. Had all the men her mother run away from been two-timing creeps like Tony? Or had her mother been incapable of sticking around, loving any man? The last thought filled Corinne with horror as she clasped the cold metal heart. I'm not incapable, she told herself, hoping it was true.

"Plus you're in shape," Sandee continued.

"Running."

Sandee raised one perfectly tweezed eyebrow. "You always were an outdoor girl."

"And bowling."

Sandee grimaced. "Don't tell me you rent those hideous shoes that everybody and their grandfather's worn."

"Okay, I won't tell you." Corinne smiled, knowing this conversation was totally grossing out Sandee, who probably wore gold high heels to church—if she went. "You look great—what do you do to work out?"

After swiping a flame-red hair out of her eye, Sandee winked saucily. "I like indoor sports."

Corinne wanted to say something glib, make it seem that she, *Conspicuous* Corinne, liked indoor sports, too. But she'd never had the chance to discover if she was good at that particular sport. Based on Tony's double-dipping, she was obviously a disappointment. How stupid she must have looked to him, sheathed in freezer wrap, when he opened that door...come to think of it, he never even checked out her sexy, see-through ensemble. His gaze never left hers...wow, Corinne McCourt goes all out to made her man howl and he doesn't even whimper...

"Hey, Earth to cuz," said Sandee, concern darkening her eyes. "Whatever you're thinking, honey, let it go. He's not worth it."

Corinne nodded, not trusting herself to speak.

"Good," Sandee said softly. "'Cause I have an idea and I think it's gonna work out swell." Sandee tapped the tip of her cigarette on a ceramic ashtray with the words "Circus Circus" in bright crimson script around its white perimeter. "Here's the deal. You need a place to stay and I need a favor."

Corinne's antennae went up. She sensed "Sandee Trouble" just like when they were teenagers. Back then, Corinne did favors like sit in for Sandee in classes while she played hooky, play waitress at Sandee's job while she partied, and once—one gloriously magical summer evening—she filled in for Sandee on a date that Sandee had accidentally double-booked. Fortunately, the guy had only met Sandee once, so he didn't know the look-alike cousin wasn't really the girl he'd asked out. An anxious Corinne had worn one of Sandee's skimpy shifts and slathered on her makeup and perfume—something intoxicatingly spicy called "Forbidden."

Corinne remembered shaking as she squirted the stuff on and shaking even more, later, when she experienced her first kiss. A mouth-tingling, mind-melding, twenty-minute lip-lock whose memory, to this day, turned her insides liquid.

"So what d'ya think?" Sandee said.

"Is it forbidden?" Corinne asked breathily. She grinned as though she were teasing, but with a jolt, she knew that's exactly why she'd come to Vegas. To be dramatic, uninhibited, forbidden. To spend two weeks being the furthest thing from the old, goody-goody, Inconspicuous Corinne.

"Forbidden? More like fun and easy money, honey!" Sandee grabbed Corinne's hand and led her to the couch. "Take a load off—I'll bring out some snacks and we'll discuss the specifics."

Corinne sank into the overstuffed pink-and-tangerine-striped couch and watched Sandee sashay out of the room, her shorts barely covering her behind. And at the end of those long, tanned legs, her bright pink manicured toes were wedged into a pair of fuchsia, sequined high-heel sandals.

Corinne smiled. Maybe her cousin's clothes were abbreviated, but her style was unabridged. Always had been. As Sandee had always boldly proclaimed, life was too short to hide your best assets.

So what were her best assets? Considering she'd worn see-through plastic and Tony's gaze hadn't slipped *once*, she was left a bit clueless. She raised one leg, and checked out her calf. The muscle was nicely molded from her daily runs. She ran her fingers up her thighs, firm, to her tummy, flat. She tilted her head and sighed. The tummy she'd once wished would soon be round. "Well, you're not gonna be round for a while," she whispered.

When her stomach growled, Corinne realized she hadn't eaten since that pit stop in some small town near the Utah border where she'd grabbed a bag of chips and a soda. Reminded her of the nights she sat up waiting for Tony, munching on a pretzel or a carrot, not wanting to spoil her dinner because she figured they'd still eat the stew—or lasagna or casserole—that'd been sitting lukewarm on the stove the last two-plus hours. After a few more pretzels, Corinne would give up and go to bed. In the morning, Tony would apologize, claiming he'd had a late business meeting with a client.

"A frizzy blond-haired client," Corinne murmured. *How could I have been so naive?*

Click click click.

The staccato of Sandee's heels brought Corinne's thoughts back to the present. She looked up as her cousin crossed the faux wood floor of the small dining room, carrying a white wicker tray piled high with food and several pop-sized bottles. Corinne could finally walk straight in her stilettos, but it would take some practice for her to simultaneously carry trays of food like Sandee. That girl was multitalented.

"Egg rolls," explained Sandee, pointing at some crispy fried cylinders with her rose-tipped index finger. Her finger waved over the rest of the items, like Vanna White gesturing over letters. "A chili relleno, chicken nuggets, some carrot sticks and two Mai Tais." She set the tray on the glass coffee table next to a stack of women's magazines.

Sandee then plopped herself onto the couch and uncorked one of the bottles with "Maui Zowie Mai Tai" embossed in purple letters on a shiny label. She toasted Corinne with a short "Here's looking at you, kiddo," took a sip, then began talking rapidly. "So, here's the deal, I got this job at a local casino…"

Corinne uncorked her own Mai Tai and tasted it, liking how it fizzled sweetly on her tongue. She settled back into the cushy couch, eager to hear one of Sandee's life stories.

"And then this dude Hank enters my life," Sandee

continued, picking up an egg roll. She paused, her blue-lined eyes misting over as she looked at the roll. "Reminds me of a baby bird he picked off the asphalt once. Little thing must have fallen out of its nest. Hank—we was driving past—lurches to a stop, hops out, and picks up that little bird. Big ol' semi barely missed Hank as he carried that little feathered creature across the road to safety." Sandee sniffed and set the egg roll back onto the plate. "For a guy with a record, he has such a soft heart," she whispered, her voice choking.

Sandee, crying? Could this Hank guy be the one who twisted her heart? Corinne handed her one of the cocktail napkins, then sat quietly while Sandee dabbed carefully at her eyes, expertly wiping away her tears without mussing her makeup. Corinne was way impressed. When she cried, she needed a mirror and multiple tissues to do damage control.

When Sandee gained control of herself, Corinne quietly said, "We don't have to talk about this."

"You kiddin'? Honey, this is part of the deal. You need to know what's happened." Rolling back her shoulders, Sandee cleared her throat and continued, "Hank was a lightweight contender years ago. He works as a bouncer now, but he's mostly on standby, so his paychecks get sketchy."

Sandee wiped her fingers on a cocktail napkin with "The Mirage" printed diagonally across it. "On our second date, Hank starts tellin' me I'm 'the one' and his heart is mine forever. I'm used to stuff like that on maybe the fourth or fifth date, but on the second?" Shooting Corinne a can-you-believe it look, Sandee took another sip of her Mai Tai.

Yes, Corinne could believe it. Sandee always had that effect on men. Even when she was fourteen, the year thirteen-year-old Corinne and her mom moved to Texas. Shy, quiet Corinne had at first been aghast at her cousin who wore tube tops, skintight jeans and bright-red lipstick that matched her hair. And when the two of them walked down a street, Corinne couldn't believe the number of catcalls and whistles Sandee got. It was like walking through a human jungle.

"So this Hank fell for you," Corinne said, enthralled with sultry Sandee's power over the opposite sex.

"Bam!" Sandee snapped her fingers. "Like a megaton of bricks. So after the second-date dinner—steak and candlelight, Cuz, none of that cheap stuff—when he takes me for a ride outside town, I figure the guy's gonna pop the question." Sandee took another sip of her Mai Tai while wriggling her perfectly plucked eyebrows at Corinne.

"So?" Corinne asked, feeling thirteen again as she listened to her wild, sexy cousin tell forbidden tales.

"So he pops all right!" Sandee slammed down her bottle. "Pops the rear end of some shiny antique car! Now we're off the side of the road, it's dark, and Hank and some old dude get out to exchange insurance info."

Corinne was wanting illicit tales of lust and love, not cars and insurance. Hiding her disappointment, she helped herself to the last spicy wedge of relleno, waiting for the rest of the story.

"Suddenly," Sandee said, her voice dropping to a dramatic low, "Hank opens the back door and shoves this old guy's limp body into the car! I yell, 'What the hel—?'" Sandee blinked. "Anyway, I yell some stuff, then Hank yells back, 'Cool it. You drive this car back to your place. I'll meet you there.'"

Corinne almost choked on the relleno. "You—" She coughed. "You drove some dead guy back here?" She looked around, half expecting to see a leg sticking out from underneath a chair.

"He wasn't dead." Sandee rapped her lighter against the thick glass top of the coffee table, the tap, tap, tap adding dramatic suspense. "I get to a stop light near the Strip and Mr. Back Seat suddenly comes to life, hops outta the car and runs like hell. The light turns green and I floor it. Last thing I need is Mr. Almost-Dead flagging down a cop and pointing at Hank's car, which yours truly is driving!"

Corinne waited. But instead of explaining further, Sandee began adjusting her top so both boobs bulged the same bulge amount. This was a woman who knew her priorities.

"So," Corinne finally said, "is that the end of the story?" Although with Sandee, one never knew the *real* story.

Sandee, satisfied she was bulging appropriately, stopped her adjustment and leveled Corinne a look. "And the end of Hank! He keeps calling, calling, but I want nuthin' to do with a bump-and-run dude. Especially when he endangered me over an old Studebaker!"

Corinne only heard the words "bump and run." The term Sandee had used on the phone. "What's does, uh, 'bump and run' mean?" Corinne took a quick, involuntary breath in anticipation of the answer. It had to be as fiery as the color of Sandee's hair.

"It's..." Sandee lowered her gaze, suddenly preoccupied with one of the sequins on her fuchsia-pink sandal. "It's nuthin' really."

Just like her cousin to avoid the question when she was up to no good. Definitely "Sandee Trouble," but Corinne didn't care. She was aching to know. "Bump and run" had to be better than any chapter in *How to Make Your Man Howl*. Probably a book in itself! "Tell me more," she whispered, almost losing her voice in her thrill-drenched state.

"I gotta split town," Sandee said matter of factly.

Not exactly the "more" Corinne wanted. But before she could elaborate, Sandee began speed-talking again.

"After that crazy stunt Hank pulled, I gotta put some distance between me and him, which is where you come in. You can stay at my place—there's a garage for the Ferrari. All I ask is you fill in for me at work."

Corinne scuffed one stiletto-heeled foot across the rose-pink carpeting. "Fill in?"

"I'm so new there," Sandee said, waving her hand as though this was the itsiest-bitsiest favor in the world, "nobody even knows me! Just show up on time, do the gig and split. I'll be gone only a week or two—just enough time for Hank to cool his burners. And speaking of lover boy, he probably won't show up at work, but if he does, just tell 'im to get lost. Considering we only had a few dates, he'll easily believe you're me. Tell 'im you got a hankerin' to be blond if he asks. And he wouldn't dare show up here 'cause my neighbor is The Phantom. You know, that hunky, mega-body star wrestler."

"Oh, good," Corinne said, her voice breaking on "ood." Mega-body star wrestler? This was so dangerous, so delicious, she shivered. "I could use the money." And the adventure. Heck, maybe she'd get a tattoo, too. Hello Angelina!

"Yeah," Sandee agreed, arching an eyebrow. "This could work."

Work. What was this job? Knowing Sandee, it could be anything from lion tamer to exotic dancer. Corinne better fess up about her minimal job experience so Sandee didn't over-estimate her cousin's abilities. "The, uh, only thing I've done for the past five years is payroll invoices for Universal Shower Door."

"Perfecto!" Sandee stood, tugged on the bottom of her shorts, as though that did any good, then picked up the tray and sashayed back into the kitchen. "Shower doors are a lot like modeling. Not much between you and the world."

"Modeling?" Corinne gulped. "I, uh, haven't had a whole lot of experiencing doing that…"

Sandee paused at the door to the kitchen and flashed a grin. "It'll be a breeze, sweetie," she cooed before disappearing.

From the kitchen, Corinne heard the refrigerator door click open and shut. "I'll take you there, show you what's what."

"Where's there?"

"Boxing ring."

3

"HERE TO SEE MY WOMAN," Leo mumbled, shooting a smug look to the squat dude playing security guard at the MGM Grand back entrance. After years of being a Vegas detective, Leo knew all the front, back and sideways doors to the swankiest places—and all the front, back and sideways lines to get into them. Tonight was an amateur boxing match, so security wasn't tight. No need to pretend he was a promoter or a manager. Just play a swaggering, cocksure boyfriend.

The guy grinned. With that puffy face and missing tooth, not a pretty sight. "Thought Red was Hank's gal."

Red. Jackpot! Hank? *That was a surprise card.*

Leo spat an expletive. "She's always full of surprises," he grumbled, shoving past Squatty as though Leo were going to straighten this out, pronto. He strutted down the dark hallway, recalling the dressing rooms were in this general vicinity, all the time listening for following footsteps. None. Cool. The enraged boyfriend act had always been a good fallback for surprise cards.

After the warmth of the Vegas summer air, the chill of the air-conditioning was like a jolt. Sharpened Leo's senses. And attitude. The clothes helped. Tonight he'd dug through his closet and picked a pair of faded jeans...he had to cool it with the Twinkies. He'd had to suck it in to get the zipper up—didn't help that Mel watched him, cackling.

Leo had thrown on a black ripped T-shirt that showed off some of the old brawn. Now that he was kicking Twinkies, he was starting to lift weights again. Dom was watching Leo closely. Leo could smell real work coming up. Real work meant being in shape—no brawn, no detective job. Sometimes the world was black-and-white.

He'd let his beard grow the past few days—it went with the "here to see my woman" look, but damn, this new beard itched. And tonight he hadn't bothered to comb his thick brown hair. Bushy hair, bearded face gave him an edge...a guy needed that edge to swagger backstage at a boxing match. Either you fit in or you were out. Black or white.

Leo scratched his chin. He checked the hallway to the right. It looked familiar. Years ago he'd busted some punk on a drug charge back here. If Leo remembered correctly, the hallway led straight to the dressing rooms...in one of which he'd find the "oversized redhead" who stole the old guy's Studebaker. He'd forgotten to ask which part of the redhead was "oversized"—the hair, the...?

Whichever, he'd never known a young oversized redhead—or brunette or blonde—to bump and run. One of the older scams. A favorite of the quick-for-the-buck con who had a few connections and didn't like it messy.

The Studebaker owner, an old guy named Willy, had said he'd been bumped on the outskirts of Vegas and after pulling over to exchange insurance information, he'd been sucker-punched. When Willy came to in the back seat of his car, he'd seen "Red" driving the car belonging to the guy who'd punched Willy out. Besides the pretty face and fire-engine hair, he'd caught a look of some "mile-long, bronze legs."

That didn't exactly narrow down the suspects considering tan, long-legged redheads were a dime a dozen in Sin City. Hell, his ex had been one. His stomach flinched as though he'd been punched. *Don't think of Elizabeth. You went through the last year of hell because she distracted you on a job—don't let her do it again.*

He forced himself to mentally switch gears, recalling the incidents that led up to his playing angry boyfriend backstage at the MGM. The old guy, Willy-something, had jumped out of the car at an intersection, then called the police and filed a report...but luck had been on his side. Two nights later, here at the fights, he'd seen the redheaded bump and runner, wiggling her bikini'd bumpers around the ring, holding up the numbers for each round.

Bingo. Easy collar.

Leo would check the dressing rooms, corner the "oversized redhead" and Dom would give Leo the chance to lead a *real* case again.

Pretty pathetic to steal a Studebaker over, say, a Beemer. No matter how long he'd been in this business, he'd never figured out people's tastes. Leo stuck a toothpick in his mouth and strutted down the hallway. Before being shot, he'd been a two-pack-a-day man...until his stay in the hospital when he grumbled for a cigarette and some cocky intern asked if Leo wanted to spend the rest of his life breathing or wheezing. Leo tried to snort some surly response—

but ended up coughing instead. That was the day Leo switched from cigs to picks.

As he headed down the MGM Grand hallway, a mix of cheap cologne, sweat and chlorine stung his nostrils. Leo opened the first door. Dark. He tried the second. Boxes, stacked chairs. He tried the third.

A naked blonde in black stiletto heels gasped. Her gray eyes widened, the color reminding him of dark, turbulent clouds. Of how his life had felt these past long months. Fighting to keep his gaze even with hers, he mumbled, "I'm looking for—"

The rest of his sentence was drowned by a shriek as she grabbed a square of white cardboard and held it over her face.

Now, instead of staring into a pair of eyes, he was staring at the number 1, painted in black on a glaringly white square, at least two-feet wide.

To hell with eye contact. He dropped his gaze. Those breasts weren't the usual fake round numbers one normally saw in Vegas. These were full, pert. Like ripe pears. The pink buds tightened as though touched by his gaze. Damn. He hadn't touched a woman's body in so long, his hand twitched as memories of stroking satiny, perfumed skin gorged his senses.

He shifted the toothpick to the other side of his mouth. He meant to finish his question, ask about the redhead, but he couldn't stop staring. Maybe because it was so surprising to see a woman with natural curves, with skin that glowed fresh and pink with no damn tan lines. The kind of skin that smelled faintly like pineapple or apples, and felt like silk under a man's tongue...

"Don't look!" she squealed, shifting the "1" to cover her breasts, which he didn't have the heart to tell her he'd already seen. Hell, memorized. And in his mind, stroked and fondled...

"Sorry," he mumbled around the toothpick, feeling about as unsorry as he'd ever felt in his life.

With a second squeal, she realized her bottom half was still unveiled, so she shifted the sign so it covered her thighs. It was a strain, but he maintained steady eye contact, unsure what she'd do next with that cardboard square. He didn't have to wait long. As her chin quivered, she raised the sign to again cover her face, as though too humiliated for him to see her emotions.

He meant to not look further, to give her some room, some respect. But he'd been born a man, not a saint. It would have been easier to stop the sky from falling than stop his gaze. It fell languidly over flushed skin, noting the shadow indentation along her collarbone, and how her pulse throbbed in that sensual hollow at the base of her neck. Her breathing was rapid. He lowered his gaze another notch. Her breasts heaved with her shaky, uneven breaths.

The lady was nervous.

And, unless he'd lost his every last male instinct, excited.

Her reaction threw his into overdrive. He shifted his stance, determined to get out...after all, a thoughtful man, a gentleman, would leave.

Unfortunately, he'd never been either.

His gaze traveled to the curly triangle between her legs. Some distant corner of his mind registered that the color didn't match the hair on her head. The thought faded, replaced by more pungent memories.

He dragged his tongue along the inside of his cheek, remembering the sweet, wet tang of a woman's perfume....

You're here for business, buddy, not a body inventory.

With an aching reluctance, he lifted his gaze back to the big number "1" that blocked her face.

Corinne's knees trembled. Partly out of fear—the only man who'd ever seen her with her clothes off was Tony. And, to be totally honest, she also trembled with excitement. Criminey, she'd never been in the same room—much less, *naked*—with a guy who looked like a rugged Mel Gibson with a surly, sexy attitude like Billy Idol.

Her knees had gone beyond trembling—they were wobbling. She tightened them, pressing the balls of her feet deeper into the toes of the high heels she'd practiced walking in all day. *I should have locked the door! Too late now. At least if she kept her knees rigid and remained standing, she'd be all right. Don't topple over, don't topple over.* She didn't *even* want to think of the view she'd give—sprawled in an extremely unladylike pose underneath ceiling lights that could double as interrogation lamps.

She peeked over the top of the board and caught the top of his unruly, chestnut-brown hair. It was wild, untamed—like him, no doubt. Throw those piercing green eyes into the mix and he made the term "bad boy" seem mild. She'd never been this close to such a man. She could almost feel his heat, his need...

...his *staring* at her body as though he had every right to peruse every inch of her nakedness...

Corinne groaned inwardly and leaned her head against the white board she held in front of her face, torn between covering her body or her face. But if she lowered this board, he'd see her look of utter humiliation. And at this very moment, seeing her emotions felt *way* more revealing than his seeing her uncovered body.

She recalled several days ago when she stood in the foyer of her home, wrapped in see-through plastic. She had been teetering in these same damn heels then, too. But she'd made the mistake of staring into the man's eyes, the man she was supposed to marry, and saw within his self-absorbed, cold gaze that he didn't really love her...

A man she couldn't go back to, which was her only alternative if she didn't pull this Sandee-gig together. Pull her wits together in front of this stranger, which is *exactly* what Sandee would do. No squealing for him to leave, no grabbing for her robe, which right now Corinne hadn't the vaguest where'd she'd tossed it. She sucked in a fortifying breath. What would sassy, sexy Sandee say at a time like this? "May I help you?" Corinne squeaked.

He paused. "I'm, uh, looking for...something."

His voice, unlike hers, was in control. Rock-bottom husky with a rough edge that sent involuntary chills rippling through Corinne. Jeez, she'd never lost it like this with any man—even her fiancé! She tightened her knees even more to ensure she remained standing upright. She glanced down and caught his feet. Big—was what they said about big feet true?—encased in a pair of worn sneakers. Above that, she saw a few inches of well-washed, roughened denim. Big, rough, with enough bad boy to make her never want to be good again...

The board was quivering uncontrollably, like the rest of her body. She gripped the edges harder, praying her sweaty palms didn't lose their hold. That red nail polish she'd borrowed from Sandee was probably melting under this sexy guy's scrutiny.

She cleared her throat. "Well, I'm the only something here." Forget sassy and sexy...it took all of Corinne's strength to sound somewhat normal. "And I need to get dressed." *Like that's a news flash.*

"Mind if I look around?"

"Haven't you seen enough?"

A low, throaty chuckle was her response. Rather than the insidious feeling she'd experienced standing near naked in front of Tony and his bimbo, this man's sexy chuckle said way more than words. Said he found her desirable. Her skin flamed hot. Probably a lovely shade of needy, I-haven't-had-sex-in-two-months, take-me-now-now-now pink. Hell, with such visual clues, the sign might as well say, "Caution! Love-starved woman." She tightened her knees harder.

Had Leo seen enough? Hell, no. A long buried primal urge wanted to see, taste, feel more so damn bad he thought he'd internally combust. Had to stop scoping out the babe, finish scoping out this room, and leave. "My buddy's wife—she works here—thought she left her purse in one of these rooms." A reasonable excuse considering lots of women worked here—from showgirls to waitresses. Plus women always related to the purse thing.

"Make it fast. I have to get—"

"Dressed. I know."

Damn shame considering she looked mind-melding

hot in nothing but a pair of heels. He scratched his chin and forced himself to look around. One black rayon workout bag. One silver-beaded purse. For a fleeting moment, he wondered about the different sides of her personality—a no-frills workout bag and beaded evening purse. Athletic *and* glamorous? Not your typical Vegas showgirl-model type.

Forget the babe. Check out the room. Nothing else indicated anyone else had been here. He debated whether to ask if she'd seen another girl, someone called "Red," but decided that might show his hand. Time to split.

"Not here," he croaked. "Wrong room." Fighting the urge for one last look at pink flesh, he backed out the door.

After shutting it, he leaned his head against the wall and blew out a gust of pent-up angst. He pulled the broken toothpick from his mouth—when had he bitten it in two? Damn he'd lost it in there. Wrong room? *Wrong reaction.* That blast of white-hot need tearing through his insides was the last thing he needed...

...and the first time he'd experienced it since his wife had betrayed him nearly a year ago. "To hell with Elizabeth," he murmured, pushing off the wall. If any thought sobered him up, fast, it was of his ex. Focused back on work with a cold-edged intensity, he retraced his steps, scanning the halls for any stray long-legged redheads even while sensing he wouldn't find her out here.

"Find Red?" asked the security guard as Leo walked past him into the hot, steamy Vegas air.

"Nah." He stared up at a cloud that floated over the moon's face just like the sign had covered the lady's.

"Like you said, man, she's always full of surprises."

"Yeah. I said that." The cloud eased past the moon, slipping into the inky blackness. *Surprises.* He pulled another toothpick out of the pocket on his T. Something had been wrong in that dressing room—but what? He slipped the pick into his mouth and began working it as thoughts tumbled over each other. No clues as to anyone else being there...the lady had definitely been alone...

Mentally, he grazed her image again...up her long, sinewy legs—the kind that made a pair of heels not just great, but killer. His mental journey halted on her navel, wondering what it'd be like to tongue that teasing indentation, before mentally moving up, past those luscious breasts...

If he had to ID her, he'd describe her body more than her features, which had been hidden behind a sign most of the time. Although during those fleeting moments when he'd been forced to make eye contact, he'd caught those curvy lips, slicked with that same searing red as her nails. Pert nose, the kind that probably crinkled real cute when she laughed.

If she ever laughed. That broad seemed pretty damned serious, and scared, for a showgirl. And then there was that mane of glossy blond hair, so shiny it almost looked metallic.

He whipped the toothpick out of his mouth. *Blond hair?* He grinned. Hell, there was his clue. If he hadn't been riding his hormones back there, he'd have put two and two together and realized he'd found his mark. The curly hairs between a lady's thighs never lied.

That lady's were a delectable crimson.

CORINNE STARED AT herself in the full-length dressing mirror. "I think the plastic wrap hid more," she murmured, staring at the black string bikini that covered the essentials, but barely. Thanks to those wedgie cupthings in the top, her breasts had leaped across the alphabet, from "Bs to Ds" as Sandee had said. Corinne wasn't just hanging out, she was spilling! *It'll be good when Sandee gets back*, Corinne thought anxiously, *because playing sex bomb is out of this girl's depth!*

The bikini bottom was almost worse than the top. The triangle that covered her privates was smaller than one of the cocktail napkins she found stacked all over Sandee's apartment. The rest of the bikini was string. Stretchy rayon strings that crossed her thigh and tied in bows on her hipbones.

She'd tied those bows so tight, she could feel the double-knotted, supertight knots boring into her hips. She'd checked out the ring earlier and even though she'd be strutting above people's heads, she didn't want some bozo running up and pulling one of those strings. Exposing herself to one stranger was plenty— but exposing herself to a roomful of strangers? She wouldn't just tighten her knees, she'd tighten her whole body. The first living human being to experience rigor mortis. She'd have to be *carried* off the stage, like some kind of bikini-clad mannequin.

"And for the rest of her life, Sandee would have to hear about it," Corinne said, giggling nervously.

The giggle escalated to a laugh. People thought she was Sandee Moray, not Corinne McCourt. Even if the worst happened, people would think it was Sandee who'd been carried out, not Corinne. Extroverted, wild Sandee—no one would believe it!

"That's me," Corinne said, meeting her gaze in the mirror. "Extroverted, wild Sandee!" A thrill raced through her, zinging her insides. When in her entire boring life had she ever been given carte blanche to act as wild and sexy as she wanted? To be a bonafide sex bomb? Never! Tonight, it wouldn't matter if someone pulled a string—or if the whole damn bikini fell off—because after Corinne left Vegas, no one would ever know it had been her.

Realizing she would survive the very worst that could possibly happen filled her with a giddy confidence.

Looking at her reflection, Corinne stepped to her right, then pranced a little in her heels. "If I feel like prancing, I can." She shook her butt. "If I feel like shaking my bootie, I can." She shimmied and tossed her head back. "If I feel like doing the come-get-me shimmy I can!" Suddenly, Corinne stopped as a realization hit her. Maybe she'd been inconspicuous because she'd never felt the freedom to be anything else. Tony had been so possessive, so jealous, that she'd retreated into herself, always trying to figure out how to please him. Blaming herself if he got mad or moody. Reading all those stupid books because *she* felt responsible for *their* relationship...books with stupid titles like *Making Your Man Happy* and *101 Ways to Get Your Guy to Say "Yes!"*...were just concrete signs of her insecurity, her putting Tony's self-centered ego before her own self-esteem.

Hell, if there was any book that had helped her with their relationship, it was *How to Make Your Man Howl* because it made her stay home that day and face the truth.

Corinne smiled knowingly, and a little sadly, at her reflection. "Being forced into this crazy situation— pretending to be Sandee—is probably the best damn thing that ever happened to mousy, Inconspicuous Corinne!" she whispered, feeling the truth right down to her core.

Knock knock. "Five minutes, doll."

Had to be Robbie G, the guy who managed this part of the MGM. Sandee had said he expected her to be punctual and sexy. Corinne was definitely the former, and she hoped the latter. "Be right there," she called out in her best sexy-as-Sandee voice.

She breathed deeply and gave herself one last once-over. Bikini bottom was tied. Breasts were spilling. Makeup was bright, unsmeared. And to top it off, she'd brushed and teased her blond mane into a wild, frothy hairdo that would fit a "Sandee."

She swiveled and strutted to the door. "I'm the one who should've been nicknamed 'Tiger,'" she murmured, ready to face the crowd.

But more than that, ready to face the rest of her life.

4

FOR LEO, AFTER SPENDING most of the past year alone, sitting in the midst of this loud, frenzied crowd was like jumping from the frying pan into the inferno. Before the accident, he'd have felt comfortable in this scene. Dug the noise, energy, and if not on duty, he'd have savored a cold beer and cursed at the fight like the rest of 'em.

And he'd have had Elizabeth at his side. His wife, the woman he adored. Hell, worshiped. His buddies had always good-naturedly jibed him, joked that Leo was "whipped" whenever he ducked early out of a card game or a drink at the bar. But he loved every moment of it 'cause he knew they were so jealous, their organs were green. Jealous because he, Leo Wolfman, was the luckiest bastard on the planet Earth. Great career, gorgeous sexy-as-hell wife, loving home.

But now, looking back, he wondered if any other guy in the history of civilization had ever been such a sucker.

Here he was, nearly a year and a half later, sitting in a crowd before the start of a fight, wishing that gnawing feeling in his gut would shrink, go away. Ever since he'd been shot, he'd carried this feeling like some kind of invisible wound. It'd been with him so long, it was a part of him, like an arm or leg. Sometimes, in the middle of the night, he had crazy thoughts. Wondered if he lost that gnawing pain, would he lose the will to live? Weird that some nagging, troubling feeling would have the power of life or death. As though if it weren't there, he'd have nothing to ground him.

His shrink had said such a feeling was normal after an extreme trauma. Called it part of his "suffering" from post-traumatic stress syndrome. *Suffering*. He'd finally asked her to stop using that term. He hated it. Made him sound *vulnerable* for crissake. Something he'd never been—until that drug dealer shot him point-blank. When Leo fell, wondering if the fire in his chest would be the last thing he'd ever feel, his gaze had met Elizabeth's. And in that horrible moment, he'd seen the truth.

She didn't love him.

The shrink had turned the tables on Leo with that one. Made *him* stop saying that. Explained ad nauseum that addicts like Elizabeth had problems. That she had loved something else more than anything in the world. More than her family. Or her health.

Or him.

He tore the toothpick out of his mouth and tossed it on the cement floor, as though he could rip the memories out of his head and throw them aside. He'd never trust a woman like that again. Marriage and families were for other men, not this one.

The buzz of the crowd intensified. A fighter strode jauntily down the walkway, a towel draped around his head like some kind of backstreet sheik. A small entourage, walking with the same cocksure strut, moved with him. The sheik's noblemen, claiming their right to fame with "We Got the Power" baseball caps adorning their heads and raised fists asserting that power. As the swarthy fighter ducked into the ring, a shudder of noise swept through the crowd. Then a second boxer, surrounded by his entourage, wearing "Kick A" T-shirts, strode down the opposing ramp, accompanied by loud rap. A woman in the row in front of Leo stood and yelled, "Kill 'im, Ralphie!" Her bloodthirsty ferocity clashed with her shiny beige stretch pants and silver-sequined tube top.

The woman's cry was like a cry to battle for the crowd, who unleashed a cacophony of screams and boos, as though someone had taken the lid off their primal urges.

Leo's own primal urge kicked in with a seismic jolt when the leggy blonde, the one he'd just seen naked, stepped through the parted ropes. As she leaned over, he caught a view of cleavage that made his mouth go dry. For a moment, he felt lost in the dark crevice between those fleshy mounds. And underneath that piece of black nothing called a bikini top, he knew were hidden those rosebud nipples.

She straightened. From where he sat, four rows back, he could almost catch the flash of gray in her eyes. Or maybe his mind was playing tricks. Maybe he wanted to be closer, wanted to again probe those stormy eyes, figure out her story. His gaze wandered. She looked damn hot in that nothing bikini...even hotter without it. Her hands momentarily bunched into fists. *Nervous?* A Vegas showgirl, or here called a ring-card girl, who was accustomed to flashing her wares in front of hundreds of people? But then, back in that dressing room she hadn't seemed like your generic ring-card girl, the way she shook holding that sign in front of her face.

That same sign that someone was handing her now. For a moment, she surveyed the crowd, as though sizing them up. Again, not your typical ring-card girl tactic. These long-legged babes thrived on the thrill, the flash. In all his years in Vegas, he'd never seen one of them sum up a crowd as though trying to figure out if they were friends or foes.

Then those red lips flashed a smile that was more telling than anything he'd seen up to this point. That smile was pure, real. Hell, her whole face smiled, betraying an internal sweetness that struck him harder than a left hook. It was like watching Elizabeth Hurley go Pollyanna.

The girl lifted the number high over her head and began walking across the ring, waving the number as though nobody had ever learned how to count. She seemed a bit stiff-legged, then eased into a long-legged stride that made Leo's heart pound with every step. Maybe she'd appeared nervous a moment ago, but this lady was getting *into* it. He could hardly believe her confident strut and the way her tushie swayed. And what was she doing now? *Prancing?* That little bombshell was *prancing* around the periphery of the ring, waving the sign, making the number "1" about the sexiest, steamiest number he'd ever seen in his life.

He blew out a puff of air and fumbled in his T-shirt pocket for another toothpick. Damn, he was out. He needed something to chew on. He rubbed his palms briskly together, wishing he could quell this burst of nervous energy, one of the side-effects of post-traumatic stress. If he were at home, he'd go outside and continue some remodeling task on his old Airstream trailer, his saving-grace hobby this past year. But he wasn't home, he was stuck here, so he planted his hands on his knees, the act somewhat grounding.

Focus your mind on business. He glanced at her hair, how the lights reflected off its fake blond dye job. She might have a Pollyanna, pure-as-driven-snow smile, but that hair color wasn't natural—a little secret he now shared with "Red."

This lady was a con.

Just like she'd changed the color of her hair, she'd change her story if he cornered her. He'd been here before. And Leo could out-con a con anyway. He'd just never dealt with one who made packing a bikini more lethal than packing a weapon.

She sashayed down one side of the ring, pivoted neatly on those killer heels, then walked along the ropes.

Their eyes met.

The rest of the room receded into a hazy backdrop, leaving him and the lady in a surreal space where only the two of them existed. The crowd's chaos of yells and boos ebbed into background static, replaced by the heavy thud thud thud of Leo's heart. Like an animal sensing her enemy, she eyed him with a wary look. Wary and...

...afraid?

She was doing it again. Throwing off mixed signals. First she looked sex-drenched, yet smiled sweetly. Now she acted hard-core hot, yet looked afraid. He'd cuffed and booked enough criminals that he could read every twitch and eye blink and know exactly what they were thinking, scheming. But her body language didn't add up. Just like two and two didn't make "1."

"Yo, Sandeeee!"

The baritone masculine voice shattered their world, thrusting them back into the bedlam of people and noises.

The girl blinked in surprise, turned her head. A mountain-sized guy, with a bald head that looked like a sculpted cue ball under the lights, waved at her. His body, a heaping mass of bulge, was barely contained in a T-shirt and shorts.

She smiled hesitantly. "Hi," she mouthed, then quickly swiveled away, saucily waving that number "1."

Sandee. So that's Red's real name.

After she left the stage, she pulled on a black satin jacket, with the words MGM Grand in big gold letters on the back. She sat straight, with her legs primly together, like some kind of schoolgirl. A schoolgirl wearing a bikini. Mixed signals, again.

Of course. She's a con. She's pulling one over on you.

And *nobody* pulled one over on Leo Wolfman.

It was part of the challenge, part of the game. For the first time in months, Leo felt his senses sharpening. Cons were smart, but Leo could be smarter. Just like he used to do, he was gathering data, analyzing the situation, planning the kill.

The Wolf was back.

"YOU TIGER, YOU!" Corinne stared at her flushed face in the dressing room mirror. She blew a strand of glossy blond hair out of her thickly mascaraed eye. "If only Tony could have seen what Not-So-Inconspicuous Corinne just did!" She giggled mischievously. "Mr. Killer Smile wouldn't be smiling now if he'd seen his mousy fiancée strutting her—" she shimmied her behind "—stuff in front of total strangers!" A year ago she'd worn a too-short skirt—or so Tony had claimed—and he'd scolded her for dressing inappropriately.

"If that was inappropriate, wonder what he'd call this?" Corinne checked out her bikini'd reflection. "Indecent? Flagrant? Brazen-as-all-get-out?"

Feeling brazenly liberated, Corinne held her hands over her head and danced in a small circle, marveling that she'd dared to wear this thing in public. And marveled how men had behaved.

While sitting ringside, waiting for the rounds to end, grown men had acted like love-struck teenaged boys! With all that attention and flirting, no wonder Sandee oozed confidence! Corinne stopped dancing and acted out some of the come-on lines. Swiveling one way, she asked in gruff voice, "Hon, can I buy ya a drink?" She swiveled the other way and responded, "Sorry, never drink on the job." She swiveled back. "Baby, we had to turn up the air-conditioning 'cause of you." She turned the other way, "Then you should be cooled down by now."

And through it all, she'd acted like her cousin, smiling that mysterious smile, forcing some huskiness into her voice, behaving as though the compliments were just part of a night in the life of Sandee Moray. And what a life! Filled with wild clothes, brazen jobs, and all those male eyes, focused on you...

Corinne halted, remembering one pair of eyes that had unnerved her.

It had been before the first round, when she'd seen the guy who'd "accidentally" entered her dressing room earlier. She'd barely hit her stride in that ring when their gazes slammed into each other. The impact felt like a collision, and it had seriously shaken Corinne's pumped-up confidence. He sat almost ringside, like a die-hard fan, yet he hadn't acted like one. While everyone else had been yelling and drinking, he'd been quiet. Hunched over in that black T-shirt, looking dangerously disheveled with that scrub of a beard and unruly hair. And his gaze had been unwavering. Zeroed in on her, *only* her. She'd had the unsettling feeling that she was the reason he was there...

No, she *wanted* to be the reason.

She wanted to be so hot, so alluring, that this mega-hunk of a guy would prowl to the ends of the earth to find her...

And when he did...whoo boy...together they'd roll off the edge of the planet and discover their own private paradise...

Corinne flapped her hand limply at her face as though the feeble action might cool her flushed cheeks. After taking a deep, sorta calming breath, Corinne whispered, "Okay, reality check. The guy's following me. Why?"

What had he said earlier in this dressing room? That he was looking for a...purse? She forgot whose purse. His girlfriend's? Well, he sure didn't seem like a man with a girlfriend. Not that she was an expert on such things. After all, she'd had no idea her husband-to-be had a girlfriend! No, the man in the crowd didn't seem attached to anyone or anything. So, forget the purse line. This guy had loner written all over him.

She shuddered, remembering his intense stare. For an instant, when their eyes locked, she'd felt more naked than she'd been earlier in this room. Maybe because he looked at her as though he knew her. As though he were *waiting* for her. It had been eerie in that ring to look out in a sea of faces and sense someone was there solely because of you. "Maybe he's one of Sandee's former boyfriends?" Corinne whispered to herself.

She'd only warned Corinne of one recent flame, the overly smitten Hank. But Sandee had also mentioned Hank's dark curly hair—which didn't match the stranger's unruly brown locks. And Sandee had also mentioned her neighbor, the overly protective "Phantom," some kind of wrestler. "Could he be the wrestler?" Corinne whispered, conjuring the image of the man in the crowd. He'd looked rugged in that body-hugging black T-shirt, a younger, badder version of a Harrison Ford maybe, but hardly a wrestler.

So who was he?

"Just some ring-card girl groupie," Corinne decided, trying not to feel disappointed that he wasn't pursuing only her. "The guy probably prowls backstage, using that purse line on any unsuspecting girls not quite fully dressed." She glanced at the door, double-checking that she'd locked it. Yes. Good. Although the thought of him entering, watching her, filled her with an electric need that took her by surprise. She'd *never* felt this way with Tony, not even when they'd first been dating. It was as though some secret part of her had come alive—the secret part that desired wild, hot, roll-on-the-floor-take-me-now passion.

She exhaled deeply. "Well, any woman who's gone without for two months would probably find any man exciting!" Darn Tony anyway. Never acting as though she were sexy, desirable. And Corinne always blaming herself, trying to figure out how to make her man howl. Confronting the mirror as though it were her ex, Corinne planted her hands on her hips. "And you thought you had a hot babe with that dumpy blonde? Bet you never dreamed that tonight a number of men—*many* men—treated Inconspicuous Corinne like a hot babe, too!"

The memory of that blonde brought back a rush of hurt and disappointment. So what if twenty men had flirted with Corinne tonight—the one man she'd entrusted with her heart, her future, had betrayed her horribly. In her mind, she heard Sandee's advice, "Don't think of the jerk. Stay busy." Corinne yanked a tissue out of a box and began wiping off the red lipstick.

But no matter how much she wiped, she couldn't wipe away the dream she'd had for so long. To be part of something bigger—a home, marriage, children. She tossed the tissue aside, then rubbed her fingers aimlessly over her tummy. She smiled sadly at the coincidence that again she was standing in front of a mirror, rubbing her round-less stomach as she had five days ago. Corinne's gaze traveled along the edge of the mirror. "At least this one's hung straight."

On a release of breath, she rolled back her shoulders. "Take it as a sign. Before, the mirror was hung crookedly, just like your life. But now you're on a straighter path…to somewhere. So what if you didn't get the home, husband, and babies you wanted… better to have discovered the truth than to have lived a lie."

Time to get dressed. She untied the bikini top as she let go of what might have been.

LEO TAPPED THE STICK against the trunk of the palm tree, wondering when in the hell Red was leaving work. Women. Always took forever to get dressed. How long did it take to remove a Band-Aid-sized bikini—a very thin, almost covering-nothing bikini—and slip into regular clothes? Maybe Sandee was taking so long because some bozo was trying to make time with her backstage. Or worse, some bozo had walked in on her while she was trying to get dressed.

Or undressed.

A surge of fire shot through him. He didn't like that some up-to-no-good jerk might invade her privacy. Okay, Leo had invaded her privacy, but he'd been up to good. And even when he had a hot thought or two, he certainly hadn't acted on it the way some other jerk might. Leo hit the trunk harder with the stick. She better have locked that dressing room door. The way she shook when he'd accidentally walked in, she didn't appear to be exactly well-equipped to protect herself. Hell, despite being naked, a more seasoned woman would have used one of those skyscraper heels to defend herself.

Leo rolled his tongue against his cheek, analyzing the situation. Nah, she was safe. Security patrolled those hallways. And there were surveillance cameras everywhere. One scream, and she'd have five burly guys in there, pronto. The lady was safe.

Safe, and mighty-fine looking...

The memory of her, barely hidden behind that sign, played mean tricks on Leo's body. He shifted slightly, wishing his jeans weren't so tight. But this discomfort had nothing to do with his love affair with Twinkies. If he'd stop thinking about that woman, he'd feel a lot better. If he stopped remembering her pink, fresh-scented body. Or those soft, perky breasts. And those legs! Damn, he hadn't seen a real, live woman's body, *naked*, in so long, he was losing it.

Unlike the former Leo. Before he'd been shot.

Back then, Leo saw more than his share of naked, curvy flesh. Being a detective in Vegas meant stake-outs that included low-class strip joints, streets where the prostitutes outnumbered the tourists. Even stake-outs inside some of the flashier Vegas hot spots— the Phoenician, Circus Circus—where tight-bodied women wearing headdresses and sequined G-strings strutted the stage with well-manicured grace.

But the body he'd seen back in that dressing room had been different. Better. It had been *natural*. And if he remembered correctly, there'd been a beauty spot right next to her navel...

Snap!

He looked down at his hands, surprised to see the stick broken in two. Muttering a curse, he tossed the pieces aside. They hit the asphalt and rolled to a stop. He'd found the stick in this corner of the MGM Grand parking lot where he stood partially hidden in the shadows of a bunch of palm trees. If he'd had a tooth-pick, he would've been rolling that in his mouth, but being fresh out he'd needed something to work while waiting. So he'd picked up a stray stick, and for the past thirty minutes, he'd been peeling, tapping and eventually tossing it while waiting impatiently for Red.

Red?

Sandee!

Stroke of luck that he'd heard that monster-sized bald dude call out to her. Funny, he'd acted happy to see her—and she'd acted surprised, maybe even a little confused, to see him. Leo shook his head. That lady gave off more signals than a radio station.

After that, Leo had watched Sandee as she sat on the sidelines or pranced around the ring between rounds. She'd studiously avoided looking directly at him after their little stare-down. Smart. She knew he was on to her. He liked a good game of hide and seek. It sharpened his predator instincts.

Patting his pocket, even while knowing it was empty, he glanced at the darkened asphalt where that stick fell. He needed something to chew, roll, fidget with. "I should take up smoking again," he grumbled.

"G'night, honey!" The squat security guard's voice broke the night quiet. "Save some o' that sweet stuff for me."

Leo stepped deeper into the shadows of the palms and observed her. Sandee wore a loose shift that floated in chiffony pink around her form, her long, bare legs terminating in a pair of heeled sandals that made sharp click click click sounds as she walked across the lot.

A light breeze traced the air, causing that flimsy fabric to cling to her shape like a jealous lover. As she headed toward him, he caught more details. Like how the loose material grazed her thighs, stroking, touching them with slow, rippling movements. Closer, he saw her firm breasts jiggle with each step. That damn shift was worse than a bikini.

As she stepped into a pool of light from an overhead lamp post, he swore he saw her pert nipples straining against the material. Those dark pink tips he recalled too vividly from their earlier meeting. Women like that should be forced to wear bras. At the very least, filmy shifts should be outlawed…starting tomorrow…

A light snap snap snap distracted him. Belatedly, he realized he was pulling on his watch clasp, opening and closing it, over and over. He halted the nervous movement and pressed his hand over the latch, wishing the cool metal could temper the hot ache below his belt.

Don't forget she's a con. Like Elizabeth.

That thought, especially the last part, swung him back to reality. He zeroed in on his prey, watching her with the cold calculation he was once famous for.

Sandee had stopped, cocking her head as though listening for something. Leo held his breath, wondering if the sound of his damn watch clasp had carried through the late-night calm. At fifteen or so feet away, in this corner of the lot, it was possible she'd heard. Especially if her senses were on alert, which was second nature with thieves. Like cops, they had to always be aware, be listening, watching. Hidden by these trees, and their shadows, he was fairly certain she hadn't seen him. But to be on the safe side, he casually leaned on a nearby car, as though it were his, and glanced up at the skies. Like a man waiting for someone, with lots of time to kill...

Watching a fiery star positioned ten o'clock to the moon, he listened intently. Quickened steps. Silence. She'd halted. For what?

Holding his stance, he shifted his gaze. Twenty feet away, she stood between two cars, one a greenish four-door Toyota Tercel, the other blocked by another bunch of palms. Her head bent, she fumbled for something in her bag. The moonlight did crazy things with her hair. It glossed over the golden strands, finding hints of red. *Yeah, red's her real color. The reason the security dude called her Red.* She pulled something out of her purse. Jangling. Keys. Leo waited for her to open the green Tercel. No. She turned to the other car...

Leo pretended to adjust the antennae of the vehicle he leaned against, in the process stepping forward to better see his mark. In his peripheral vision, he caught her opening the driver's door of a...

Ferrari.

His body tensed as though an invisible cold front had just passed through this particular corner of the world. It washed over him, leaving him edgy, sharp. He watched as she eased herself inside a shiny yellow Ferrari, pulling her shift neatly underneath her like some damn lady going to tea.

The door clicked shut, the sound reminding Leo of the chamber of a gun snapping into place. His gut flinched. Old habit.

As the Ferrari's headlights turned on, pointed away from him, he cautiously stepped from behind the group of trees, keeping one eye on the Ferrari as he sidled over to his Mustang. Quietly, he opened the door and slid into the driver's seat.

When the Ferrari eased out of its parking space, Leo turned the ignition key. He paced her, waiting until she was several rows of cars away before he followed. Then he kept his distance, driving slowly through the parked cars, using them as cover. It was like hunting, singling her from the pack.

Yeah, the Wolf was back.

5

CORINNE'S STOMACH growled like a wild beast. She glanced at the digital clock display on the Ferrari's dashboard. 11:45 p.m. "Well, no wonder," she murmured, easing her foot on the brake as she braked at a stop sign. "I haven't eaten since lunch, which was yet another feast of leftovers." To be exact, a handful of nuked pizza rolls, a glass of apple juice and several slices of jalapeño cheese. She'd hoped those green flecks were jalapeño, anyway.

Later, after practicing her high-heeled strut for the last time, she'd been too nervous to eat dinner before driving to the MGM Grand. She was afraid she'd squeeze into that bikini and bulge in all the wrong places or she'd be sashaying around the ring and double over with a tummy ache. Either way, *not* the impression she wanted to make her first big night as a ring-card girl.

Her stomach rumbled again. "I hear you," Corinne said, shifting into first. "But as Sandee would say, 'Here's the deal.' Although I don't mind *pretending* to be Sandee, I insist on eating *real* food again!"

Ever since Corinne had arrived in Vegas two days ago, she'd eaten only what was available in Sandee's kitchen, which consisted of some containers of frozen food, a variety of mostly identifiable leftovers, and some birthday cake from a party Sandee had gone to.

When Corinne had asked whose birthday, Sandee wasn't sure, but said she'd had a great time.

That was Sandee, all right. The life of the party, even if she wasn't sure whose it was. And as far as a kitchen filled with leftovers, well, that was Sandee, too. She'd never been domestic. She'd once watered a plant for two months before realizing it was plastic.

But enough was enough. Now that Sandee had split to whereabouts unknown—with the promise she'd call by tonight!—the kitchen belonged to Corinne. And she was going to buy some *real* food, cook it and eat it. She could almost smell the tomato-rich pasta sauce, the steamed and lightly buttered spinach. And for dessert, she'd have fresh berries with a dollop of whipped cream.

Her stomach responded with a low, prolonged roar. "Hello to you, too!" she responded. "Keep growling like that and I'll end up writing 'How to Make Your Stomach Howl.'"

She smiled at her little joke. But the smile widened as she realized she was miraculously finding humor in her new quirky life. Totally unlike the old Corinne, who didn't laugh so easily over life's bumps. She'd always taken her self-imposed rules to heart—like never being late to work, never opening her blouse past the second button, never asking for things she really wanted. Never never never. "No wonder life felt tough," she said quietly. "I lived in Never-Never Land."

A mentality due, no doubt, to always moving as a kid. With her mom constantly getting engaged or married, and her home constantly changing, she'd made up a zillion little rules to give her life shape. Some-

thing she'd still be doing if she hadn't caught Tony
with that bimbo.

She felt a funny tickling inside, an almost happy
feeling. "Well, I'll be," she whispered. "I never
thought I'd feel *grateful* for discovering Tony's infidelity." But she did. Otherwise, she'd still be living in
Denver, pretending things were fine, pretending she
wasn't miserable. This had to be what her pal Kyle
called an "ah-hah" moment!

Corinne looked out the tinted window at the hazy
Vegas sky and its twinkling lights. *A week ago, if someone had told me I'd flash my naked self to a total stranger
and prance in a bikini around a Vegas boxing ring, I'd have
pointed them to the nearest mental health clinic.* Because
Inconspicuous Corinne of Never-Never Land would
never, never have done those things.

But now that I have, anything is possible!

She smiled to herself, loving the rush of exhilara-
tion. "Like, at this very moment, finding a supermarket!"

She was only a few blocks from Sandee's apartment—and hadn't her cousin said there was a supermarket two or three blocks away? Of course, Sandee
wasn't sure as she'd never actually *shopped* there, but
swore she'd driven past it on several occasions.

This was a fairly busy street, so Corinne took her
chances it had a supermarket on it. Sure enough, in a
few minutes she spied a large, well-lighted building,
its parking lot sprinkled with cars and metal shopping
carts. "Guess other Vegas-ites do their grocery shopping at midnight, too," she murmured, swerving
neatly into the entrance. "Whoa, this baby handles
well!" she exclaimed, then mentally kicked herself for

not choosing a better word. *Baby*. Tony's nickname for this Ferrari. Irked, she hit the gas pedal and zipped toward a parking lane.

Screech. Honk. "They drive like that in Colorado?" yelled a gruff male voice.

She braked and glanced over at the stopped white Audi. A very grumpy looking man sat behind the wheel, the scowl evident ten feet away. His arm, hanging out the driver's window, gestured in a not so gentlemanly manner.

"Make that 'flash my naked self to a total stranger, prance in a bikini around a Vegas boxing ring and get flipped the bird in a parking lot,'" she muttered. The old Corinne would have felt terrible, apologized, maybe tried to exchange insurance information even though nobody had been hit.

Not the new Corinne. She hit the window button on the console. It rolled down. She leaned forward so the man could see her face and flashed him a big smile. "No," she said, putting some Sandee ooze into her voice. "In Colorado, we drive even wilder." Then she gunned the motor, *twice*, before moving on.

A few minutes later, she eased into a parking spot close to the front of the store where there were plenty of lights. After all, this was a very expensive car—fifty grand, plus the numerous fixes and tune-ups worth hundreds, sometimes thousands, more. She only knew because Tony had constantly rattled off the cost of every tune-up, brake job, even car wash for which he'd had to shell out money to keep his car in primo condition. And Corinne always quietly listened, never mentioning she'd like a few extra bucks to do this or that because she knew it would tick off Tony if he felt she was asking for too much.

But Baby? Different story.

Corinne removed the key from the ignition. Sandee had left her several hundred dollars—a down payment for Corinne's upcoming "modeling" job as the official paycheck would be made out to Sandee Moray, not Corinne. "Well, tonight, I'm gonna blow some big bucks on groceries! Get a jar of marinated artichokes, some fancy-shmantzy goat cheese, a package of homemade pasta, not that dried-out stuff..." With thoughts of overpriced food dancing in her head, she stepped out of the car.

Outside, as she pressed the button on the key ring to automatically lock the doors, she stopped and glared at Baby. "What did he see in you?" she snapped. "You're nothing but a sleekly packaged engine with fancy metal. Just like those...those women he fools around with. But do you have a heart? Can you love? Can you have a baby, Baby?" Corinne swallowed a lump of hurt, while fighting the urge to go over and kick the hell out of Baby.

LEO FIDGETED WITH VD, twirling the charm between his thumb and index finger, as he watched Sandee standing outside her Ferrari, yelling at it as though it had just insulted her. Women. Go figure. You'd never see a *guy* arguing with his Ferrari. Hell, it would be his best bud.

But then, the car obviously wasn't hers. Pretty ballsy, though, to be driving it around to public places like casinos and supermarkets. Even ballsier to stand in a public lot, arguing with it! This con had an attitude bigger than her strutting, sashaying, prancing act in the ring, which said a lot.

As she pivoted neatly and made a beeline for the store, Leo hung VD back on the rearview mirror. Its round wooden head, the size of a golf ball, bobbed at the end of the string. With the feathers exploding off the sides of its head, it looked like a mini-Pinocchio gone punk. After Elizabeth cleaned him out, even taking the car, he'd scraped together a down payment on this ten-year-old GT Mustang, which ran okay, but wasn't Leo's dream car come true with its grinding brakes, flashing airbag light and faulty power steering.

And then he'd found this strange feathery object under his front seat when he'd taken it to the carwash for the first time. At first he'd thought it a bald chipmunk, then realized it was some kind of wooden thingamajig with feathers sticking out of it. After the crash and burn of his life, he decided it was a good omen. Hell, even if it wasn't, he needed a good omen. He decided it was a voodoo doll, using its powers to ward off evil spirits. And brother, had Leo seen his share of evil. He could have named his new pal "Voodoo," but shortening it seemed more appropriate. And so was born "VD."

"Hang tough, VD. Be right back." Leo eyed Sandee through the glass windows of the store. For a con, she sure played easy to get.

He didn't buy it for a minute.

CORINNE PUSHED THE cart more slowly than she usually did. But then, she didn't usually go shopping in the middle of the night wearing a gauzy shift and high-heeled sequined sandals. No wonder Sandee never went grocery shopping—it was darn near impossible to walk on these slick linoleum floors in heels. One slip and you'd end up face-down in some food section. Hopefully, not the frozen food section. Corinne shivered, imagining what it'd be like to have a carton of ice cream stuck to your forehead.

"Don't think about high-heel disasters," she murmured to herself. Now that she had the down payment, plus some money still left from Kyle and his pals, she should buy herself a pair of sneakers or running shoes. Maybe Sandee could live her life in heels, but Corinne needed to come back down to earth occasionally. Besides, she missed her morning runs.

The thought of reclaiming a piece of her life, a piece she *enjoyed*, filled Corinne with a moment of happiness. As exhilarating as it was to pretend being Sandee, it was grounding to recall bits of her self, too. Like jogging. And eating real food.

Classical music played through overhead speakers, which struck Corinne as funny. Sin City plays classical music in its supermarkets? Who woulda thought? She hummed along with a trilling violin solo, vaguely recalling a Mozart tune she'd wrestled with on a violin when she was ten. That had been during her mom's marriage to Terence, who didn't seem to like anyone, including Corinne and her mom. One day he up and left. Corinne's mom had cried nonstop for a few weeks. About a month later, she announced they were moving from L.A. to Salt Lake City, where she'd found a job.

Corinne hadn't really cared about the new job, she just cared that her mom wasn't crying. And, selfishly, she was glad she didn't have to take violin lessons anymore. If I ever have children, Corinne thought, they'll live in one home, with only one dad, and no music lessons unless they want them.

She looked into her basket. Organic tomatoes, a jar of marinated artichokes, fresh linguini, butter, garlic, a bundle of spinach...so far, so good. Now where would they keep some of that fancy-shmantzy goat cheese?

Wheeling along, she looked up at one of the signs that hung over the food aisles. This one listed items like paper products, light bulbs, baby items...

Baby items.

A force compelled her to turn the cart and head down this aisle. She stopped first at the jars of baby food, each imprinted with the cutest babies' faces. Happy, cherubic faces that grinned at you as though nothing bad had ever happened in the world. She wheeled past a row of baby lotions and powders, then stopped. Picking up a bottle of baby oil, Corinne pulled up the plastic top, and raised it to her nose. Its light, sweet scent conjured images of soft, pink baby skin. With some reluctance, she put the lid back on and set the bottle back on the shelf.

I should go. Lurking in the baby aisle is like a chocoholic lurking in the candy aisle. No, worse. What chocoholic loved chocolate more than anything else? She pushed the cart a few feet then stopped. Neatly arranged on pegs were teething toys, teeny-tiny bibs, baby cups...little, precious baby items.

I should go. But the thought faded as she picked up a white rattle with a picture of Tweety Bird on it. She gave it a shake. The sound was muffled, more like a hushing sound than a rattling sound. She imagined a baby cooing or giggling at the sound—its little round face looking like one of those cherubic images on the baby food jars. She shook the rattle again, enjoying the hush-hush sound it made.

If she had a baby, she'd shake the rattle and entertain the little one. Oh yes, she'd be a fun mom, the ways hers could be when she wasn't weathering a breakup. In Corinne's house, there'd be lots of laughter and little fingerprints and scattered toys. And she'd play with her kids, encourage them to hold on to their imagination, and to never retreat to Never-Never Land.

She shook the rattle, then did a little side step, dancing in time to the shushing sound of the baby rattle.

LEO CHECKED HIS wristwatch. Sandee had been dawdling in that aisle for a full fifteen minutes now. Sniffing this, shaking that, but not putting a damn thing into her shopping basket. Prior to now, she'd scampered around as though she were still free-wheeling in that Ferrari, snatching vegetables and grabbing boxes of stuff with the zeal of woman on a mission.

And what a visually appealing mission, too. Leo hadn't suffered too much on this part of the stakeout as he watched that gauzy shift hug and caress her body under these bright lights. She'd slipped once or twice in those contraptions called shoes, but managed to catch her balance. What was it with women and their shoes? Had to be the eighth wonder of the world.

But now, it appeared, she'd found an aisle that grabbed her attention, big-time. She'd sniffed and fondled and played with things as though she were a kid.

At first he'd been annoyed, then intrigued when she

started to dance as she shook something in her hand. She'd been sexy dancing around that ring earlier, but now she looked dreamy, lost in thought as she swayed from side to side. He'd been electrified by her at the ring, but mesmerized here in the store.

And, surprisingly, he also felt a little guilty. Something the Wolf never felt when he was on the hunt. But with this woman, he felt as though he were invading a very private place. Plus here, her movements were innocent, like a girl's, which put a new light on Leo's impression of Sandee. What moved her to feel something so deeply in a supermarket, of all places?

"Excuse me," said a gravelly voice. Leo looked down at a seventy-something woman with tan skin, pink-white hair, and a shirt that read Bite Me. "You're blocking the soy milk."

"Sorry." He moved over, trying to stay positioned behind a table piled high with boxes of crackers and cheese. He was nicely hidden back here, between the table and a refrigerated section, which he now realized contained products like rice milk, soy ice cream, and tofu burgers. Man, it was like a sixties food flashback.

"You're still in the way." The older lady made a disgruntled sound.

If he moved, Sandee would see him. Recognize him as the guy in her dressing room, the ring, and now the supermarket. No, he had to stay put. He glanced at the soy stuff. "What do you want?"

"You work here?"

"No. But I'll help you anyway."

She squinted, as though debating whether to trust this man with her soy request. She must have seen *something* trustworthy in Leo's face, because after a beat, she sucked in a breath and began rattling off, "I want some organic soymilk, fortified with beta carotene, vitamins B-12, E, D and calcium."

Now it was his turn to pause. "Is that one item or a dozen?"

She made that disgruntled sound again. "One. You're not into soy, are you?"

"No, I'm a Twinkies guy myself." Ignoring another disgruntled sound from her, he scanned the cartons on the shelf. "Here it is."

"I want the vanilla flavored."

He gave her a double take. "All those vitamins...and you want it vanilla flavored, too?" But before she could say "Bite me," he checked out the soy cartons again. Yes, there was one labeled organic, advertising a slew of vitamin names, with the word "vanilla" mixed in. He handed it to the lady, who took it without a thank-you and walked away.

"What is it about me and women?" Leo grumbled, turning back to watch Sandee.

She was gone.

He darted from behind the cheese display, checking out the immediate area. Damn. He should've stayed in the parking lot, waiting for her to return. But in case she'd noticed him tagging her, he didn't want her slipping out a back door of the store, so he'd followed her inside.

He took a few giant strides to the right, certain she'd have headed in this general direction—after all, she'd adopted a very precise, systematic way of shopping, starting from the left and heading methodically to the right. He was ready to bolt toward the exit when he spied that telltale shift.

Sandee.

Leo stopped, heaved a calming breath and watched her as she pushed the cart down the magazine and book aisle, scanning covers and titles. No problem. He'd head down the aisle she'd just spent forever in. If he stood toward the end of that aisle, he'd have a clear view of the other end of the magazine aisle, where she'd be exiting.

Besides, he was curious what had captured her attention so completely in this aisle. He headed past some picnic items, snatching a box of toothpicks in route, scanned boxes of plastic utensils, paper plates, followed by cartons of...disposable diapers. He grimaced, kept walking. She'd been about here. He stopped and looked at the rack of baby items.

Little cups with cartoon characters, pink and blue-bordered bibs, little spoons with the biggest handles he'd ever seen. And in the midst of all this, he spied what she must have been shaking.

A baby rattle.

Big, white, with a yellow bird face on it. *What was that bird's name, anyway? Oh yeah, Tweety.* He looked into Tweety Bird's big, blue innocent eyes—astonishingly like Sandee's, although hers were gray. He glanced at the end of the magazine aisle. No Sandee, yet. He looked back at the rattle. So why had she been shaking a baby rattle and dancing? He surveyed the rest of the items, the little shirts and toys she'd been consumed with. Yet didn't buy. What kind of woman did that?

A woman who wants a baby.

He wasn't sure if this insight made him happy or pissed him off. He'd wanted a baby, bad, with Elizabeth. Hell, he'd even talked about it on their first date—nearly asked her to marry him then and there when she'd claimed to want the same. For a guy who rarely gambled, he thought he'd hit the jackpot—he'd lucked out and met a drop-dead gorgeous gal with a great sense of humor, a love of life and best of all, she wanted kids. Lots of 'em.

But after they got married and he'd wanted to get serious about making babies, she'd stalled. Said the timing wasn't right. He'd badgered her, reminded her how much it meant to him, and she finally gave in. A few months later he found the birth control pills.

He'd said a few things he later regretted, but the disappointment never really left. Truth be told, which she didn't seem able to do, she never wanted children. Just another dark detail he wished he'd known about Elizabeth before saying, "I take you as my wife..."

Leo scrubbed his hand across his beard, refocusing on the present. Ever since being shot, he tuned in to his emotions too quickly, too strongly. Right now, he felt anger, mixed with a yearning that hurt right down to his bones. *Forget the past. Stay focused on the present.* His therapist's words crept up at times like this, reminding him how to go on living. Go on working.

Click click click. Sandee pushed the cart out the end of the magazine aisle, turning away from Leo as she headed toward the checkout.

Good. He'd head to the express line, at the other end, then be out in the parking lot, in his car, before she left the store. As he hunched over and walked in the opposite direction, the slap slap slap of his rubber-soled sneakers against the linoleum reminded him of the muffled sounds of that shaking rattle.

THUMP. THUMP.

Corinne stopped stirring the sauce and listened. What could that be? She checked the clock on the stove. Nearly 1:00 a.m. Maybe it was the neighbors—

Thump. Thump.

No, that was close. Sandee's front door? At this hour? Corinne turned down the sauce and tiptoed to the edge of the kitchen linoleum floor, holding the wooden spoon stained with red pasta sauce. Reaching the edge of the living room carpet, she stopped.

Thump. Thump.

Yes, that was definitely someone knocking—well, thumping—on Sandee's door. Whoever it was didn't want to be ignored. Although she was relieved Sandee had left a message tonight on the phone machine—a number where she could be reached, the promise she'd be back within the week—Corinne was a tad anxious to be playing Sandee *outside* of work, too. But considering the circumstances, she really didn't have a choice.

She started into the living room and hesitated. She'd never really checked out that pane of glass next to the front door—if someone was on the porch at night, could they see her clearly? Not that she traipsed around naked, but she liked to know if people could see inside. No, the glass was thick, rippled. Decoration only. The best someone could see was movement.

She crossed the plush rug, peered through the door peephole and gasped. A huge flesh-colored balloon was floating outside...or that's what she thought until it moved and two big eyes blinked at her. Now she realized it was a huge bald head.

Those eyes, that head, looked familiar.

It was the guy who'd yelled at her tonight at the ring. *Sandeeee!* Although Corinne had smiled and said "Hi," it had taken her two more rounds, staring across the ring at him, to figure out it must be Sandee's neighbor, the wrestling star known as the The Phantom. Who else would have the body of a mountain, the head of a balloon and know where she lived? Still, she'd better check to be sure.

"Phantom?" she called through the door. Darn, she should have asked Sandee for his name.

"You okay?"

"Uh, yes. Why?"

"You never call me Phantom."

She waited, hoping he'd say his real name. Nothing. She'd detour the name part. She cleared her throat and tried to put some Sandee-huskiness into it. "What's up?"

"You got a cold?"

Forget the husky. Anyway, Corinne felt confident this was Sandee's neighbor, what's-his-name. Plus, she'd said he was actually a big ol' pussycat who felt protective and mothering toward her, so it had to be safe to open the door.

Corinne glanced down at the oversized T-shirt she'd thrown on after getting home. It'd been in Sandee's bathroom, hanging on the back of the door. It had a picture of Snow White on the front, the seven dwarfs on the back. It didn't seem Sandee's style to have cutesy Disneyland clothes in her wardrobe, so Corinne figured it must have been a gift from one of her admirers. Anyway, it was wear this or something see-through, sparkly, or abbreviated.

She opened the door and flashed her best Sandee smile, the one where Sandee quirked her head a little to one side and smiled a bit secretively. Also, it was dark in the doorway, so if her smile was a bit off, he wouldn't notice.

"Sandee?" The Phantom stood on the doorstep, wearing a pair of sweatpants minus a shirt. Corinne forgot all about head-quirking and secretive smiling. All she could think was that he was the biggest mass of chiseled, bulging flesh she'd ever seen in her life! Had to be three or four heads combined. Hairless heads. Criminey, the guy shaved his chest!

She knew her mouth had dropped open, but she was too stunned to close it. Did he use an electric shaver? It could be life-threatening to use a razor over all those mounds and crevices—

"Sandee?" he repeated. "You okay?"

No. "Yeah." She forced her mouth to close.

He frowned. "What're you doin'?"

He was staring at the spoon in her hand. "Shaving—I mean cooking."

"Why?"

"Because I'm hungry."

"But you never cook."

Right. Sandee never cooked anything except a man's brains. "I, uh, decided to take up a hobby."

Honest to God, he looked hurt. That's when she noticed the pan in his hands. He'd baked something for Sandee? Corinne had never had a man cook for her. "Just a hobby," she repeated, feeling as though she had to explain herself. He still looked hurt. "Probably a phase. You know, I was curious what was in supermarkets so I bought this spoon and some...food things." She smiled. He didn't. "I'll probably take up another hobby next week. Maybe learn how to clean house."

His hurt look softened. "Okay." He thrust the pan at her. "Made you some brownies."

Brownies? This big hunk of shaved male had been in his apartment baking brownies? "Thank you," Corinne said, meaning it with all her heart, trying to remember she was cool and together Sandee while being grateful and awed Corinne. A man playing Betty Crocker? She never dreamed such things happened in the real world.

He shrugged. Which on him looked like a mountain shifting. "No big deal. Had to make 'em for my niece's birthday party—figured I'd whip up an extra batch for you, too." He blushed a little. Then it hit Corinne. *He's in love with Sandee.* But with all the male attention her cousin received, Corinne would bet her stolen Ferrari that Sandee hadn't noticed.

In a funny way, The Phantom reminded Corinne of herself. How hard she tried to win Tony's approval and love. Maybe she couldn't cure The Phantom's aching heart, nor did she want to lead him on as "Sandee," but she could show him some kindness and appreciation for his efforts. Let him know what he'd done was valued, special. Things she wished she'd felt from Tony.

She accepted the pan, holding one side of it while The Phantom held the other. "Thank you—" Uh-oh. The name thing again. She'd have to snoop around and check names on mailboxes tomorrow. She put on her best smile—quirking her head a little to the side for the Sandee effect.

His blush deepened. "W'come." Honest to God, he was shuffling his feet. This big hunk of a man, who wrestled other big manly hunks, was acting like some crushed-out boy. She held her spoon up. "I should get back to my pasta."

He stared at the spoon as though it were his enemy.

"This week's hobby," she reminded him.

He looked relieved.

"Well, good night!" she said cheerily, pulling gently on the pan as a cue he could let go. He did. She started to shut the door, when he spoke.

"Uh, what'd you do to your hair?"

"Colored it."

"Why?"

"Wondered if...blondes really do have more fun." She grinned, but The Phantom didn't. "Seriously," she said, trying to figure out how to handle this. "I, uh, wanted a change." Oh boy, was that the truth.

"Oh. Well, you look pretty no matter what color you are."

Oh-h-h. This guy had it bad for her cousin. She'd have a heart-to-heart girl talk with Sandee when she got back. At least, Sandee might find The Phantom a real girlfriend so he didn't spend his spare time pining and cooking for her, trying to win her love. "You're sweet—" She paused where one normally said a name. "Thank you," she added quickly, closing the door until it was open just a few inches. This guy didn't take hints. "Good night!" she whispered through the narrow opening.

"G'night, Sandee," he said, smitten written all over

his face. "If you need anything, you know where I am."

Unfortunately, I don't. With a feeble smile, she clicked shut the door, then leaned against it and sighed heavily. Funny, in the last five minutes, she'd gotten more affection and care than she had in the last five months from Tony. "Ah-hah," she said softly.

6

LEO SAT IN HIS Mustang across the street from Sandee's apartment, eyeing the big bald dude on Sandee's doorstep. "He looks like a walking meat-packing house," Leo muttered.

Ever since this guy had shown up, Leo'd been watching carefully to see if this late-night visitor was good news or bad news. When Sandee had opened the door, Leo had his answer. That big guy shuffled his feet and dipped his head like a geeky kid trying to work up the nerve to ask out the most popular girl in school. And if that wasn't enough, the poor guy had held on to that pan as though holding on to Sandee. She'd been gracious, holding on to her end, not acting as though it were strange that it took two adults to hold one bitty pan.

And what was in that pan? Its shallow, squareish shape, covered with aluminum wrap, reminded Leo of the numerous dishes his mom had made for school functions, neighborhood potlucks, bridge parties. Based on that piece of past evidence, Leo would swear the guy had baked something.

Baked something? "Gee, buddy," Leo muttered, "if you'd put on a shirt, you could wear your heart on your sleeve."

She'd closed the door now, but the Brawny Baker seemed unable to leave, watching her door like a hopeful puppy who hoped to still be let in. It was almost painful to watch. "Give it up," Leo said under his breath. "If the lady wanted more than friendship, she'd have taken the pan *and* you inside."

What would it be like inside Sandee's apartment, privy to her world? Leo pondered that for a moment, knowing he shouldn't go there, but lacking the willpower to reel his mind back in. What would it feel like to earn her trust, her love? Damn good, he bet. He'd seen facets of her personality that showed her to be shy, yet sexy. Sensitive, yet brassy. She was the combination of fire and soul that men dreamed about, but rarely found. He'd bet his Airstream that with her, a man would indulge himself in the sweetest life had to offer—a woman whose body could lust, her heart love...

"Whoa!" Leo flicked VD, who swung wildly back and forth, his feathered head bobbing. "Stop me if I go there again. Otherwise, I'll start reading recipes, showing up with pans of stuff." Although with Leo's cooking prowess, it'd have to be some kind of Twinkies casserole.

VD slowed to a quiver, then stilled. "That's right, keep me grounded, buddy," continued Leo. "You're my partner on this stakeout. If my mind starts steaming about Sandee again, tell me to chill. Remind me I've been without for too long—that any woman would look good. Hell, I'd probably fall all over myself for Miss Piggy."

Although Leo seriously doubted it. Truth was, he could be staking out Penelope Cruz and he'd still be daydreaming about Sandee. Something about her clicked with him on a gut level, like some kinda crazy soul connection. He chuckled cynically and slapped the steering wheel. Logical Leo, who kidded his mom when she'd gone to a psychic, or teased his buddies' wives when they talked about astrology, felt as though he and Sandee shared "a soul connection"?

"I'm holding you personally responsible for that one," he said to his feathered cohort. "Can the high woo-woo voodoo vibes. I gotta job to take care of."

Leo looked back at Sandee's front door. The Brawny Baker was lumbering back up the stairs he'd descended ten or so minutes ago. Seeing him retrace his steps, Leo surmised Mr. Baker was a neighbor. *Guy's probably okay. Worst crime is being a love-struck protector.*

Leo scanned the building, a beige multitiered mass dotted with windows. The glint of streetlamps in the squares of glass looked eerily like pairs of eyes staring back at him. For a moment, it unnerved Leo...brought back that ugly anxiety he felt, right after being shot, whenever he was around people. If it hadn't been for his therapist, Dr. Denise, he'd probably still be a recluse. When he thought how he'd sat in a crowd at the boxing ring tonight, he'd come a long way, baby.

Leo snapped on a pen light and flashed it on a matchbox cover on which he'd written the Ferrari's license plate. He'd have done this earlier, but got sidetracked observing that heartsick dude with the pan. But now Leo wanted to check out the plate number he'd jotted down earlier while tailing the Ferrari.

Using his police radio, he called the clearance channel and requested they run a check on the plate. Within minutes, Leo was informed the vehicle belonged to a Tony Borgeson at something-something street in Denver, Colorado. Leo didn't care about the address, and he already knew the car was from Denver. What interested him were two things. One, who was this Tony Borgeson fellow, and two, why was his car hundreds of miles away in Sandee's garage?

Only one way to find out.

"Get me Tony Borgeson's phone number, will ya?" He grabbed a pen off his dash and scribbled the digits underneath the license number on the matchbook. "Thanks." He ended the call, then flicked his wrist to check the time. Ten after one. He mentally calculated Vegas time to Denver time. Had to be ten after two in Denver. If it was a stolen bike, Leo would wait until a decent hour to call, but this was a *Ferrari*. Even if the guy had loaned it to Sandee—which Leo seriously doubted—he'd bet Mr. Tony Borgeson would be grateful to know the authorities were concerned about his big-bucks vehicle.

Of course, Leo wouldn't mention it was currently safely stashed in a garage, which was the only smart thing he'd seen Sandee do with the car tonight. Prior to that, she'd driven it to work, to the store. Hell, yelled at it. Flaunting stolen merchandise wasn't your typical criminal behavior, but Leo'd seen enough to know that no matter how much you thought you knew human behavior, somebody would fool you.

Even he'd fooled himself about Elizabeth.

Using his cell phone, Leo punched in Tony's number with a bit too much force. The phone rang one, two, three times before a groggy male voice answered. "Hullo?"

"Tony Borgeson?"

Pause. "Yeah?"

Leo ran the spiel, identified himself, had barely explained that he was IDing a yellow Ferrari when Tony cut in.

"Where you callin' from?"

"Las Vegas, Nevada," Tony repeated.

"My car is in frickin' Las Vegas? What the hell is it doing there?"

As a detective, Leo was accustomed to dealing with emotional people. His cool, collected side kicked in. "That's why I'm calling. We wanted to ensure you were aware—"

"Las Vegas?" Tony barked, followed by a string of expletives.

Leo waited. When Tony ran out of steam, Leo responded coolly, "That's affirmative. Your car is in Las Vegas."

"She's probably at her cousin's..." His voice drifted off. "Thanks, Officer, I'll take care of it."

Leo sat up. He wasn't prepared for this turn of events. "Was the car stolen, sir?" he probed.

This time there was a longer pause. "Uh, no."

The guy was lying. But Leo was too close to let this go. "Because if it's a stolen vehicle," Leo continued, "the police can impound it."

"It wasn't stolen."

Like hell. But before Leo could try another tack, Tony continued.

"I know who has my car. She, uh, borrowed it. I'll fly out to Vegas, take care of it."

She borrowed it? "No reason for you to fly out, I can—"

"It's my car. My property. I don't want the police involved."

Leo's hands were tied. If Tony didn't want the police involved, there wasn't a damn thing Leo could do. Didn't matter that he had a con right under his nose, with a probable "bump and run" vehicle to boot. If the owner didn't want to press charges, Leo was stuck. And this case was crucial because Leo knew, just *knew*, it led to the Studebaker bump and run. Damn it all anyway. He'd been *this* close to escaping desk hell...

"As you request, Mr. Borgeson," he said, keeping his voice level, cool. "But if you change your mind, let me give you my name and number."

"Yeah, sure."

Leo gave the information, betting Tony wasn't writing down a single word. After ending the call, Leo looked at VD. "I smell a mystery. One starring Miss Bump and Run and Mr. Denver." Leo pulled out a toothpick and bit the end. "We're not gonna solve anything at this late hour. Let's call it a night, VD, go home and sleep on it."

He started to turn the ignition key when the drone of a motor caught his attention. He glanced up and saw a Tracker, parking in front of Sandee's apartment building.

It cut its motor. A wiry, compact guy hopped out the driver's door. He wore shorts, sandals, and what Leo had always called a "pec T" because it resembled the sleeveless, low-necked T-shirts his Uncle Bennie used to wear. Perpetually tan and nauseatingly good-looking, Bennie's T-shirts flaunted his bronzed skin, chest hair, but most of all, his buffed pecs. He said the ladies liked the look, and Leo believed it considering Bennie had plenty of 'em. But after marrying curvy, tempestuous Vonnae, Bennie suddenly switched to sports shirts.

The "pec T" man jogged up the walk to Sandee's door. Stopping, he pulled a comb out of his back pocket and ran it through his curly black hair.

Leo shifted in his seat and watched. "Check it out, VD. The guy is *grooming* himself for Sandee like some kinda Latin James Dean. No food offerings. And he's wearing Bennie's tried-and-true ladykiller pec-T." Leo shifted the toothpick to the other side of his mouth. "I think we got us a real, live suitor. Maybe the boyfriend? Wanna bet he's also in on the bump and run?"

Bye-bye desk duty, Leo mused, settling back in his seat and watching...

STIRRING THE BUBBLING spaghetti sauce, Corinne again marveled at her cousin's power over men. The Phantom, a he-man, over-muscled wrestler, had baked a pan of brownies! Back in Denver, Corinne couldn't even get Tony to open a jar or take out the trash. "If I'd ever asked him to bake a batch of brownies, he'd probably have thought I meant those little girls who sell cookies."

So where did Sandee get this magical power that compelled men to do all kinds of things for her? It couldn't be *just* the bikinis and short-shorts and skimpy shifts that made men take up culinary skills. Corinne lifted the wooden spoon to her lips and tasted the spaghetti sauce. Thick, hot, with chunks of savory tomatoes. She licked her lips. *Mmm.* The perfect blend of spices and sauce.

Hmm. Like Sandee, who was a blend of spice and...*confidence.* That was it! Corinne set down the spoon and contemplated this insight. "When I first put on that bikini tonight, I was a bundle of nerves. Yet I pumped myself up and went from a scaredy cat to a Tiger! Confidence. *That's* the secret."

And another little secret she'd tried to keep from herself was how, as she strutted like a tiger around that ring, she'd relished that man watching her. The man who'd surprised her in the dressing room and knew every inch of her naked body, yet *still* watched her as though he wanted more. And knowing what he wanted had been unsettling...and damn thrilling.

With a shaky hand, she turned on a second burner to start the water boiling for the pasta. As the blue-white circle of flame burst to life, so did a hot need within her. Hotter than anything the old Inconspicuous Corinne had *ever* felt. "Interesting how acting sexy can make you feel sexy," she murmured. But to be honest with herself, tonight on that stage she hadn't been "acting." That man's blatant appreciation of her body, and that sexual glint in his eyes, had unleashed her own primal urges. When she'd strutted around that stage, she'd loved teasing the audience...but loved even more teasing him...

Knock knock knock.

Corinne blinked, hard, forcing her mind back to her immediate reality.

Knock knock knock.

She glanced at the clock on the stove. 1:30 a.m. "What'd The Phantom do now? Whip up a cake?" Sandee had mentioned that she worked late, played late like most people in Vegas, which undoubtedly meant late-night visitors as well. But Corinne couldn't keep calling Sandee's neighbor and pal "The Phantom." She had to find out his first name. Tomorrow she'd definitely check out the apartment building's mailboxes—although she seriously doubted one would say "Mr. Phantom."

With a sigh, she turned off the sauce, the water and headed for the door. "This guy's gonna make me fat for the few days I'm here," she said under her breath. She peeked through the hole.

No bald head.

No massive, shaved chest.

Instead, she saw a pair of soulful chocolate-brown eyes looking at the hole beseechingly. The eyes matched the curly, dark hair on his head. "Baby," he whispered, "open up."

Baby. Just for using that word alone Corinne was ready to walk away, back to the spaghetti sauce that at this moment offered more warmth and comfort than any man possibly could.

"Baby, I'm sorry," he said in a husky, needy voice. He was so close, she saw the diamond stud earring in his lobe and the low-cut T-shirt that revealed a mass of curly, black chest hair. Antonio Banderas, step aside!

"Listen to me, *mi amante,* I can explain." She heard a light brushing sound. Was this hunk of magnificent male *scratching* at the door?

Criminey! Sandee had 'em cooking and begging!

"Baby," he continued in that low, pleading tone. "I didn't mean to make you bump and run..."

Bump and run! This had to be Hank, the guy who stole—and broke?—Sandee's heart! Corinne pressed closer to the door. What would Sandee say? She'd been pissed, big-time, at Hank. He's the reason she'd escaped Vegas for a few days, to get away from *this* guy. Corinne sucked in a deep breath. "Go away or I'll call the police." She blinked rapidly, amazed she'd stood her—well, Sandee's—ground!

More scraping sounds. "Honey, I don't blame you for being mad. But please listen to me, that's all I ask." He murmured something, sounded like Spanish, in a deep, velvety tone that made Corinne's skin tingle. Damn. No man had ever spoken to her like that! Maybe, for Sandee's sake, Corinne should continue listening...

"After I lost my job at the Grand," he said, "I was desperate, baby, *desperate* to make money. Fell into my old ways. I was wrong, wrong, wrong. Not only did I compromise my integrity, I lost you."

Corinne's mouth fell open as she watched him thump his fist against his hairy chest, punishing himself for the pain he'd caused Sandee. Oh-h-h, this was better than Antonio in any movie...

"I'd do anything, baby, *anything* to win back your love. You were my sun, my moon, my..."

Corinne had heard enough of what Sandee was. If this guy loved Sandee so much, why'd he break her heart? This Hank was like other men, like *Tony*. Come to think of it, they even looked alike with that dark Mediterranean coloring—one Italian, the other Spanish. Corinne always knew she and Sandee shared a common bond but until this moment, she hadn't realized they also gravitated toward the same type of man. Dark, charming, and selfish as all get out. Men who thought nothing of betraying you, then had the gall to expect you to welcome them back with open arms. With a surge of anger, Corinne yanked open the door.

Hank reeled back, then squinted. "This porch light's bright, baby. I can't see you in there—come outside."

"No." She liked standing in the shadowed area inside the front door. She liked the power of watching him, but his not being able to fully see her.

Clasping his hands together, as though he were praying, he looked at her with those melting chocolate-brown eyes and sighed, "You opened the door, so you've also opened your heart."

"No," Corinne answered coolly, "a door isn't my heart. It's just a door." Okay, not exactly the most stellar comeback of all time, but she'd warm up. After all, this was her moment to avenge Sandee, to tell this guy what a louse he'd been. Criminey, it was Corinne's opportunity to avenge herself, avenge all women! And wasn't it karmic that she was doing it at a front door— the same setting where her own heart had been broken less than a week ago. Now she could be strong, tough, make some no-good, scum-dog hear the truth.

"Baby—"

"For starters, no more baby talk." She should have said that to Tony years ago. Made him name that Ferrari Geraldine.

Hank snapped shut his mouth and blinked at her. "But you always like it when I called you that—"

"Not anymore." She crossed her arms over her chest. Would Sandee do that? Well, she did now. "And I don't like that you did me wrong." Okay, she didn't know the specifics of what happened between Hank and Sandee, but that line covered a lot of ground.

Hank dropped to his knees. Bowing his head, he crossed himself and murmured, "I'm sorry."

Sheesh, this guy was dramatic. Plus he *apologized*—something Tony would never have done, for anything! Plus from this vantage point, looking down on a mega-hunky guy on his knees, begging for forgiveness...well...it was a miracle Corinne could remember how to breathe, much less figure out what to say.

What would Sandee say? Corinne paused, thinking back to when she'd seen Sandee argue with one of her many boyfriends—but that was when they were teenagers. Sandee had probably cultivated a lot of great zingers by her adult years.

Sensing her hesitancy, Hank lifted his head. His brown eyes were watering. Was he going to cry? Where did Sandee find these baking, sensitive men?

Hank swiped at his eyes. *"Te amo."*

Te what? "I don't know what that means."

"Yes, you do," he answered, his voice breaking. "I said it on the night I proposed to you. The night I swore to you my undying love for the rest of our days, our children's days, our grandchildren's. *Te amo.* I love you. If it takes the rest of my life, I'll do anything, anything, to make it up to you."

Undying love. Our children. Corinne felt some place inside of her, some deep hidden place, start to soften. Where before she'd been angry, now she was feeling a tad anxious. Just like the night at the Grand when she'd worried she was out of her depth squeezing into Sandee's bikini, she was starting to worry she was out of her depth playing Sandee with Hank. This guy was getting to Corinne with his words. Words she'd yearned to hear Tony say. It was becoming tougher and tougher to pretend being strong, in-control Sandee...maybe Corinne should stop, retreat back into herself...

On the other hand, this might be the only time in her life she'd ever hear such a heartfelt confession of love. And maybe she was pretending to be Sandee, but God help her, she wanted to live this moment, hear those things, vicariously know what it was like to feel cherished, loved.

And she wanted something else.

"Why did you do it?" she whispered, saying what she'd ask Tony if he'd ever had the decency, the integrity, to own up to his deceit. The question she'd never get to ask, but always wonder about.

Hank thumped his fist against his chest again. He shook his head, opened his mouth, then shook his head again as though the burden was so great, it was unspeakable. Corinne let her gaze wander over this man her cousin had fallen so hard for. She'd never thought of Sandee as passionate. Sexy, flirtatious, fun? Yes. But die-hard, lusty, no-holes-barred passionate? Not really. Yet, looking at this Hank, who yearned for Sandee's forgiveness, who was man enough to display his intensely powerful love for her cousin, Corinne *knew* Sandee had experienced a profound passion with this man.

"I—I wanted a future for us," he finally said.

Hardly the response she expected. But whatever he'd done must have been bad, or else Sandee would be here on this doorstep dealing with Hank. But Corinne also knew her cousin still loved Hank. She'd seen it in Sandee's eyes, heard it in her voice. Maybe Corinne could do something to help?

Unfortunately, at this moment, she hadn't the vaguest what that might be.

So she stood, arms still crossed, and let her gaze travel over him. His skin was rich in color, like caramel, and dusted with dark wisps of hair everywhere she looked...along his arms, his neck, his chest, his legs. The wisps of black matched the thick curls on his head, which glistened underneath this stark porch light. And when he looked up, she was astonished that such a strong face housed such tender, brown eyes. And with those ample lips and that sparkling earring, the man looked like a swarthy pirate.

Sandee sure knew how to pick 'em.

But he'd hurt Sandee, she reminded herself. Broke her heart. Be strong for her. Speak up for her. "How can there be a future after what you did?" *Whatever that was.* "It's too late, Hank." Now she wasn't sure if she was speaking to Tony or Hank, but the ultimatum had already slipped out.

That pleading look came back into his eyes. "Don't say that, *mi amante*," he whispered, his voice breaking. "I'd do anything to win back your love. Swim the deepest ocean. Climb the highest mountain. Fight my way through a tycoon..."

She was fairly certain he meant typhoon, but the guy was on a roll. Plus, selfishly, she wanted to experience a slice of this passion. To virtually be Sandee, wallow in a moment of a man's heart-wrenching expressions of love. Because she might never be this close to it again...

Instinctively, she stepped forward, onto the porch.

Hank looked up, eagerness lighting his eyes. "Baby—I mean Sandee—" He stopped and gave her a funny look, his thick black eyebrows rising. "What happened to your hair?"

"I...colored it." He stared at her so long, she panicked. Did he notice something else? Realize she wasn't really Sandee?

"Colored it?" He looked perplexed.

"You don't like it?" Even as she said the words, she could have kicked herself. It was like asking approval from Tony all over again.

"No."

She wanted to say something back, something sassy like Sandee, but at this moment she was just Corinne. Now she knew how Cinderella felt when her gown turned back to ash cloth.

A shadow fell over Hank.

She looked up. There stood The Phantom, his bulging, hairless arms crossed over his bulging, hairless chest. The scowl on his face was like watching an approaching thunderstorm.

"There a problem here?" he asked in a rumbling, baritone voice.

Corinne made a mental note to write The Phantom a thank-you note for those brownies.

Hank turned his head, his perplexed look changing to confusion, then anger. He jumped up, but even standing, his head came to the middle of The Phantom's chest. Corinne held her breath, waiting for Hank to say something apologetic again—which anyone in their right mind would do when faced with a monstrous, scowling mass of muscle.

"Who the hell are you?" Hank demanded.

Obviously he wasn't in his right mind.

"Who is this dude?" Hank asked, turning to Corinne, his face contorted with rage and...jealousy?

"The Phantom," she murmured.

"The *what*?" Hank said, his voice rising. He stepped closer to Corinne. "So you dumped me for this new guy? Is that it? I screw up once and you find a new boyfriend?"

Corinne hesitated, feeling her tummy do a weird flip-flop. She'd never been in this situation before—criminey, she'd never even stood up to Tony, and now here she was, expected to smooth over a brewing fist-fight between two men who were both mad about her?

Time to be confident. Corinne flashed a stern look at Hank. "Just because you came begging for forgiveness, doesn't mean I hand it out. Go home. I need time to think." She started to step back inside her apartment when she realized she'd better add something. Looking at The Phantom, she added, "You go home, too. Because if you guys get messy out here, I'll call the police."

And on that threat, she stepped inside and closed the door. Peeking through the peephole, she watched the men glare at each other for a solid minute. Finally, Hank backed off, still not breaking the stare-down. After a few moments, The Phantom headed back up the staircase.

Corinne listened to an upstairs door shut. Then, from outside, a motor chugged to life and drove off. She breathed in and out, slowly, glad the drama of the evening was over.

But when a second motor chugged to life, she frowned. Another car?

Another man?

A *third* one?

"Sandee, I'll teach you how to cook if you'll teach me how to juggle," Corinne murmured, heading back to the kitchen.

7

"HERE TO SEE 'YOUR woman' again?" The squat security guard chortled to himself as though it were immensely amusing to see Leo at the back door of the MGM Grand the second night in a row. Overhead an owl hooted from somewhere in the night skies, as though joining in the joke.

This guy needs a life beyond door guard. "Yes," Leo answered as he started to step inside.

"Sorry." The guard held up his beefy arm to block Leo's entrance. "She's not taking visitors."

Leo looked down at the arm, then back to the guard's puffy face. "Since when?"

"Since I said."

Everybody's a con, thought Leo. He pulled a twenty out of his jeans' pocket, folded it neatly in half lengthwise and held it midair.

The guard squeezed the bill between his chubby index and middle fingers. "Just trying to save you trouble," he said, grinning so wide that Leo got a better view than he ever wanted of that missing tooth gap. "You're the second boyfriend here tonight. Claimed he was a boyfriend, anyway. Wanted in, bad, but I told him to use the front door with the rest of the paying customers."

It was eight-twenty. The fight started at nine. So who'd be trying to visit Sandee backstage this early?

The Brawny Baker? Nah, Leo suspected he was protective on Sandee's home turf, but not here. Had to be the pec-T guy.

"Yeah, Sandee's a special kind of dynamite," continued the guard, slipping the bill into the pocket of his chino pants. "Man's gotta be ready for an explosion to be near her."

"Good thing I'm powder-shy," Leo said casually as he stepped past the guard. It was the truth, in a twisted way. After being shot, he wasn't looking forward to any gun action again, although it was inevitable in his line of business. Just as he wasn't looking forward to tangling with a woman again, but that too was inevitable, being a male.

And even more inevitable was his gut-deep feeling that it would be Sandee he'd tangle with, sooner or later. He couldn't shake the feeling that they were destined to ride out something deeper, meaningful. Maybe if he hadn't seen her dancing with that baby rattle, hadn't realized she wanted kids as desperately as he once had, he wouldn't have started thinking such crazy thoughts.

But maybe they weren't crazy. Maybe they were logical. *After all, Sandee fits the profile I wanted in Elizabeth, so I think there's a soul connection.* He choked back a laugh. Such thinking was a remnant of the old Leo, who believed such nonsense. Believed the world was a rainbow when actually it was nothin' more than a black-and-white picture.

He retraced his steps into the back area of the Grand, down the hallway to the right, toward Sandee's dressing room. Finally reaching the closed door, he stopped as a thought slammed into his mind.

Why hadn't the guard mentioned Hank?

Last time Leo did the "here to see my woman" routine, that guard had said, "thought Red was Hank's gal."

So it hadn't been Hank, whoever he was, who'd try to enter before Leo. Leo quickly calculated the situation. The guard didn't appear to know tonight's "boyfriend's" name, so chances were he wasn't a regular. Which nixed the Brawny Baker, who Leo guessed showed up often, not necessarily backstage but in the ring, to see Sandee. Besides, it didn't take a therapist to see that Mr. Baker wasn't a boyfriend.

Then there was Mr. Pec-T, but that didn't fit, either. After witnessing Pec-T's passionate display on Sandee's doorstep last night, and his macho act with Brawny, Leo deduced Pec-T was one hotheaded, possessive male...named Hank. But the guard hadn't said Hank's name tonight.

So this "boyfriend" had to be someone else. Someone new? How many guys did Sandee lead on?

Leo fumbled for a toothpick in his shirt pocket, telling himself that burning feeling in his gut was due to the Polish dog he'd eaten earlier, not jealousy. This is just a job, he reminded himself, popping the toothpick between his lips. Sooner it's over, sooner I get a real detective gig. Black and white.

He knocked on Sandee's dressing room door, ready to out-con a con.

Corinne looked at the door. "Robbie, I still have thirty minutes." Funny that Robbie G., the manager, would be knocking this early. Last night, he'd knocked five minutes to show time, just as Sandee had said he would.

"Not Robbie," said a deep male voice. "Leo."

Leo? Sandee hadn't mentioned a Leo. "What do you want?"

"A few minutes of your time."

That voice was familiar. "Why?" She checked that the door was locked, which she'd done tonight *before* stripping and putting on her bikini. She didn't want any surprise visitors like last night.

"Tony sent me."

A chill crept the entire length of her spine. She drew in a shaky breath. She should have thought things through better, not just run away in Tony's Ferrari. He must have called her work, her mom, Kyle...and after hearing that nobody knew where she was, guessed where she might have driven to...Sandee's.

So if Tony sent this guy, he knew she wasn't Sandee. This could be a big problem if Corinne messed up Sandee's modeling job. Plus, the MGM Grand probably wouldn't be too happy that they'd hired an impersonator. Rather than blow her cover—and Sandee's reputation—she'd best let him in.

"Let me throw something on," she said, grabbing a short, flower-print silk wrap she'd snagged from Sandee's closet. It didn't have any buttons, or a tie, but at least she wouldn't be entertaining a total stranger dressed in a red string bikini and red heels.

When she opened she door, she gasped. "You're—"

"The guy from last night," he said quietly, stepping inside. He shut the door behind him.

She clutched the robe closed with both hands, hoping he didn't notice they were shaking. "Looking for another purse?"

One side of his mouth kicked up in a lopsided smile.

"No." His eyes darkened as he quickly looked her up and down.

His darting gaze felt like shots of heat. "Didn't know Tony had friends in Vegas," she said in a distant, breathy voice she didn't recognize. Forget pretending to sound like Sandee, she suddenly wasn't sure how Corinne spoke anymore.

A distant light flashed in Leo's green eyes. His smile widened. "Yes, seems Tony has friends here...as well as a car."

Car. Tony's precious Ferrari—of course, that's what this was about. In the following silence, they locked stares like two opponents sizing each other up before battle. The only sound was the rickety hum of the air-conditioning.

Finally, Corinne cleared her throat and said, "He can have the car."

The light in Leo's eyes dimmed, as though he hadn't expected this response. He pulled the toothpick from his mouth and looked around for a place to toss it. As he turned away, Corinne checked him out. He wore jeans and a Hawaiian shirt that desperately needed ironing. And a beard that needed trimming. This guy looked as though he lived on the run. Plus, his rumpled, furry exterior was the opposite of Tony's creased, tidy appearance.

This guy was Tony's pal like she was Sandee.

Irritation rippled through her. Why was it that men thought they could always pull one over on a woman? If it wasn't the guy at the car repair shop doing a shoddy brake job, it was the guy you were living with doing you wrong. And most women didn't confront it, just took it. Pretended to believe the lies so they didn't cause trouble.

Not anymore.

Corinne analyzed this situation. This Leo fellow knew Tony's name. Maybe he'd heard through somebody else that Tony's "Baby" was in Vegas? Maybe he wanted to steal the stolen car?

Well, if he wanted to play pretend, so could she. This would be a game. A game where she could play hard, because one wrong move from Leo, and she'd yell. Robbie G would be here faster than this guy could say "Ferrari."

After tossing the toothpick into an empty ashtray, Leo looked at her. Corinne smiled sweetly, the way Sandee might when she toyed with a man. "Tony can have it back," she said, pumping enough heat into her voice to melt this guy's charade. "I told him that just the other day." With an innocent shrug, she released her grip, letting the robe fall open.

It had just the effect she wanted. Leo's gaze dipped again, only this time it didn't bounce back so quickly. Well, while he was eyeballing her, she'd give him something else to think about. She shifted one of her high-heeled feet to the side, rotating her hip ever so slowly...

His eyes shot back to hers, checking her intentions. She met his gaze and held it, challenging him. She liked this sense of power. No, *loved* it. She'd spent years denying it, hiding from it, but now it was coming out with a vengeance.

And best of all, at this moment, she wasn't pretending to be Sandee. She was Corinne McCourt. The strongest, most in-control woman on the planet.

He seemed to sense the shift in her because he changed before her eyes. Where before his stare had been direct, it now turned primal. Those green eyes smoldered as though, at any moment, he could devour her...

Her heart thundered. Fire flashed through her.

She tried to hold on to her control, but the shock of his overt sexuality ripped through her like a bolt of lightning. She felt burning and cold, all at once. The atmosphere felt heavy. Charged. She couldn't breathe. She parted her lips to take in air...

...but before she could, he moved forward and pulled her body tightly against his. His breath singed her ear as he whispered huskily, "You tease, I take." Then he crushed her in an embrace, his mouth ravishing hers in a punishing kiss.

His scent was pungent, male. His body hard, strong. His lips moved to her neck, where he burrowed his head and kissed and suckled. When she gasped with pleasure, his mouth recaptured hers with a reckless abandon. And when his hand slid down her bare stomach and kneaded her hip, she groaned out loud.

Her senses reeling, she returned his ardor with abandon, driving her tongue between his lips, exploring the hot wetness. She felt wild, out of control, desperate to taste, feel more...

Then he jerked away, holding her at arms' length. He panted, his eyes glittering with desire...

...and anger.

Stunned at his reaction, she staggered away from him, vaguely aware the wrap had fallen in a silky pool on the floor. Her body trembled so much, she clutched the edge of the dressing table for support.

Leo shook his head, hard, like an animal. Then he turned and opened the door. With his back to her, he said gruffly, "I'm sorry, Sandee."

The door shut behind him with a crisp click.

Corinne sank into a folding chair, its cool metal barely tempering her heated skin. "Sandee?" she murmured.

At some point, she'd forgotten this was a game.

LEO SAT ON THE EDGE of his seat, literally, because the fat guy next to him took up one and a half seats—the half being Leo's. *I got to cool it with the junk food,* Leo told himself for the nth time. If he didn't, he'd end up being the better half of somebody else's seat, too, someday.

He'd move, but there were few available spots this close to the ring. Plus it was an aisle seat, which gave him an easy exit in case he needed to follow the "new" boyfriend, who still hadn't materialized despite Squatty's warning. Leo's seat had an additional advantage. A few rows back from the ring, he could easily watch Sandee—and follow her if necessary. He'd mentioned the car, so she knew he was onto her. He blew out a puff of air.

Onto her was right.

He'd lost it in her dressing room, but damn it, it was her fault. She let that silky flowery number fall open, exposing a mouth-watering view of flesh. Her vital parts were barely covered with patches of red, which matched the color of his ignited libido. And then she'd slid one stiletto-clad foot to the side and done that swivel thing with her hip. It was like waving a box of Twinkies at a starving man.

A starving, pent-up, out-of-control man.

No, not a man. An animal.

He shouldn't have prided himself earlier on thinking "the Wolf was back," because he'd become one. A four-legged creature just because a woman flashed a little leg. Okay, and gyrated a nicely rounded hip. But still, he'd behaved as though civilization had never evolved, as though he were a beast, ready to devour his prey. When he'd closed that space between them, his actions were instinctual, motivated by hot, raw need.

But she'd lit a match to his fuse. Leo suppressed the urge to laugh at himself. What had he told the guard, that he was "powder-shy"? *That's a good one.* He'd thrown himself into the fire...and knew he'd do it again if given the chance.

If Dom knew about Leo's "you tease, I take" act back there, or what Leo was still feeling, he'd be knocked down from desk duty to kitchen duty, if such a position existed. Didn't matter. If Dom had his way, he'd *create* such a special position for Leo, making him fill and refill ice trays until he learned to cool down.

A rumbling chant interrupted Leo's thoughts as one of the boxers marched down the ramp with his cocky entourage, who all wore sunglasses as though their king's radiance was too bright to behold. Leo could feel the tension in the crowd increase. Clapping, whistling. Voices cried out the boxer's name, "Ben...Be-e-e-e-en," elongating it into a long whine of expectation.

The second boxer was close behind, his gang wearing so many gold chains, they looked like a walking jewelry store. Reggae boomed in their wake, encouraging a rhythmic chant of "John, John," which built in volume until the sound pounded the air.

The crowd was primed, their glee crackling through the air like a blue flame. There was something darkly sexual about people before a fight, Leo realized. All the fanfare and build-up was like foreplay, the entire room pulsating with pleasure, expecting release when the fighters finally sparred, connected, then brutally consummated their union. Although with their pairing, only one emerged victorious.

Leo shifted his gaze back to the ring as Sandee—in that daring red number—stepped one toned, high-heeled leg into the ring. Suddenly Leo felt protective, wanting to spare her the crowd's thirst for blood. Why the hell did she have to wear red? She looked like a piece of meat. His insides roiled with emotions—lust, fury—as he watched her. He felt like yelling at her, asking her what in the hell did she think she was doing?

And in a flash of understanding, Leo realized his anger was because he yearned for something more than this act she was showing the world. Yes, she was sexy. Yes, she knew how to fan a man's desires. But Leo knew she was more. Underneath his fiery need, his heart yearned for the tender woman he'd seen at the store, the woman who danced with rattles and dreamed of babies....

She leaned through the ropes, her body momentarily against the thick, taut cable, as though she were riding it....

"Hoo-boy!" exclaimed the fat guy, shifting so much in his seat he damn near shoved Leo off his. Leo gritted his teeth, determined not to overreact. Maybe this crowd was ready to rip loose, but Leo was determined to stay grounded. Especially after losing it in Sandee's dressing room, he needed to prove to himself he was together, professional, *cool.*

But it was hard to be the latter when his gaze swept back to Sandee, who'd managed to de-ride the rope and was now sashaying around the ring, waving that number card. His pulse boomed in his ears. What was that bikini made of? That thin stretchy material molded to her body like tinted plastic wrap. His palm itched as he recalled the creamy texture of her skin, the tight curve of her thigh.

He shut his eyes. *Together, professional cool.*

"Dolly, what's yer number?" yelled the fat guy, moving so much Leo had to hold on to the edge of his seat unless he wanted to end up sitting in the aisle. "What's yer number, honey?" Fatso leered, his face shiny with sweat.

"Her number is one," Leo snapped, shoving his arm against his rotund neighbor as Leo physically reclaimed his territory. And then shoving a bit more 'cause the guy irked him. "One," Leo repeated, "Or didn't you get that far in math?"

The fat guy jerked his head toward Leo, his eyes narrowing into puffy slits. "Who squeezed your pineapple?"

Pineapple? Food reference. It figured. Leo ignored what he assumed to be an insult, returning his gaze to Sandee as she strutted and pranced. He swore she'd caught his eye, flashed him a look filled with a need that mirrored his own. Maybe he was imagining it...maybe not. He licked his lips, recalling how she'd returned his kiss with a fire that shot straight down to his groin...

"I said," continued his neighbor, leaning close and yelling into Leo's ear, "Who squeezed your pineapple? She's just a..."

The noise of the crowd drowned out the last word, but Leo knew what the creep had said. In a flash, Leo grabbed the neck of the guy's shirt, bunching the fabric with one hand while curling his other into a fist, which he planted squarely beneath the bulbous nose. "Take it back," he demanded between clenched teeth.

"Man, we're watching a fight, not participating in one—"

"Take it back." Leo was borderline. Flash point. One wrong move, and this guy's nose would be next to his ear. "Take it back or I'll squeeze your pineapple until there's nothing left but pulp."

The guy's mouth fell open as he blinked rapidly. "I—I take it back."

The guy reeked of whiskey and cigarettes—funny, no pineapple—but Leo didn't release his hold on the shirt, or lower his fist, for a solid moment. He wanted Fatso to memorize the threat in Leo's eyes. Satisfied his message had gotten across, Leo dropped his hands and turned back to the ring as though nothing had happened. Amazingly, he had his entire seat to himself.

So much for "together, professional cool." Well, Leo had never liked mantras anyway. Way too much woo-woo voodoo.

He watched Sandee, who looked like a walking match in that red number, undoubtedly setting every man's fantasy on fire. He cut a look around the crowd, knowing what every other guy was thinking and hating him for it. But he didn't have the time or energy to threaten every single man in this joint.

"What in the hell are you doin' dressed like that? Get off that frickin' stage right now!"

At first Leo thought the words had come out of his mouth until he saw a guy standing at the base of the ring, gesturing wildly at Sandee, yelling at her to stop this, *frickin' now,* and get off the *frickin' stage.* Sandee froze, the number one held high over her head, as she stared, wide-eyed, at the guy.

"You're crazy!" The guy was pacing, gesturing, yelling. "Crazy driver, too! Corinne, you damn near crashed Baby on your way over here!"

Leo tensed as he quickly assessed the situation. The guy acted wild, but was meticulously groomed. Leo gave him a once-over. Through the guy's lightweight slacks and thin polo shirt, it was easy to see he wasn't carrying a weapon. Maybe he was another of her deranged admirers, his system overloaded with the possessive gene.

"Crazy driver!" the guy called out again, pointing his index finger at Sandee—or had he said Corinne?—to ensure she knew he was talking to her.

Crazy driver? Well, after the way she almost hit that Audi in the supermarket parking lot last night, Leo had to admit the guy had a point. Although what man thought about driving skills when facing a hot babe in high heels and a bikini?

A thought tore through his brain. *A man who's fixated on a car. Like maybe his Ferrari.*

Was this Tony?

Leo jumped up. Had to get down there, convince

the man to step outside so Leo could ask a few questions. Too late. Security guards appeared on either side of the guy. Leo eased back down into his seat, watching...

The guy reacted like a cornered insect. Began flapping and buzzing, making even more of a racket. People were booing, yelling. Somebody laughed raucously as a wadded ball of paper flew through the air. One of the security guards appeared to be talking to the guy, who didn't seem to want to listen. When he started flailing again, the guards went into action. One neatly pinned an errant arm at an obviously painfully angle because the guy visibly winced. They began escorting him up the aisle.

As the happy trio passed Leo, he heard the guy say, "I have a right to tell her to get off that stage! That's my frickin' fiancée up there!"

Sandee, engaged? Leo had been close enough to notice if she wore a ring, but the last thing he'd thought about was what was on her hand. Besides, she appeared to live alone, with who knew how many boyfriends, so the notion of her being *engaged* had never crossed Leo's mind.

But when he thought about her at the supermarket, fondling those toys with that mushy look on her face, well, there was no question than the woman wanted to settle down, have children.

He looked back at the stage where Sandee stood, her bare legs suggestively apart, wearing more red on her lips and nails than on her body. The woman in the baby aisle was a hell of a lot different than the woman up there on the stage. Almost as though they were two different women...

A notion starting taking shape in his mind, but before Leo could identify it, it faded to black. Damn. Before the shooting, his mind had been razor sharp, zeroing in on the truth like a wolf on the hunt. Since then, his memory and thinking skills had gradually improved, just as Dr. Denise had predicted, but he still wasn't a hundred percent and that pissed him off. *If I lose this gig...*

No, he wouldn't go there. He'd win, not lose. Black and white.

He glanced back to the ring. Sandee had resumed her strutting around the stage, but some of the oomph he'd seen moments before wasn't there. She seemed a bit...scared. Of the crazy guy? Ring-card girls were accustomed to an occasional weirdo getting too close, so it had to be something more about this guy...this guy named Tony.

After she exited the ring, Leo noticed her talking to one of the security guys. He patted her arm reassuringly. Leo didn't have to hear a word to know what was being said. *She's saying she's scared, needs to leave.* Leo felt irritated at her sweet, pitiful look. Because that's what cons were good at—playing the game, fooling you, making you empathize and care and sometimes even love them.

He should know. He'd been married to one.

Time for Leo to stake out the Ferrari, follow Sandee home. With two men tailing her, she might split Vegas. And Leo wouldn't let that happen. Not over his together, professional, cool body.

DESPITE THE THEATRICS at the ring, following Sandee and staking out her place were uneventful. She drove straight home. No visitors. Leo kept expecting the guy who lost it at the ring to show up. But after placing a few calls, Leo discovered the guy was in a holding tank for the night. Seems he slugged one of the security guards. Leo asked for slugger's name, but his resources didn't know.

Leo decided to go home. His hunch was Sandee would stay put for the night—she hadn't seemed rushed, like a person ready to split town. Plus, he seriously doubted she'd drive at this hour in that stolen, borrowed, whatever-the-story-was car. Especially with two guys on to her.

Thirty minutes later, he pulled in front of the white stucco home he'd rented almost a year ago. Everyone else on this block parked in their driveway, but he'd reserved his for the Airstream trailer. This way, he could lay out his tools in the driveway, work on the trailer when the mood struck.

Leo walked up the curving cement walkway that wound its way through a front yard strewn with decorative white pebbles. He stopped and admired his Airstream, recalling the many hours he'd spent fixing it, working up a sweat repolishing the exterior, remodeling the interior. For many months, the activity had given his shattered life cohesiveness.

And it gave him a dream—to one day jump in the Airstream and drive to a new life. That small ranch he envisioned in his mind's eye. Lots of grass and trees. No pebbles.

Leo unlocked the front door and pushed it open. A long, low whistle greeted him. "Hey good-lookin'!"

"I bet you say that to everyone," Leo said, holding out his hand as he passed his parrot Mel, whose favorite perching spot was the edge of the brown leather armchair. Mel hopped onto Leo's arm and walked up to his shoulder.

It had been their nightly ritual ever since Leo went back to work four months ago. Two lonely bachelors, preparing to spend the evening together doing lonely guy things.

Leo headed for the kitchen where he opened the fridge and pulled out a cold soda. Leo squawked.

"No, Mel. Just soda."

Squawk. "I want Merlot."

"I said no."

"Merlot." Mel hobbled down Leo's arm, walking like a miniature pirate with a peg leg, and hopped onto the kitchen counter. There he proceeded to saunter over to the wine rack, a double-layered contraption of wooden rings stacked on top of each other. Within the circles were several bottles of red wine.

Leo looked at the bottles, remembering when he'd turned to the stuff every single night. Sometimes mornings and afternoons, too. He'd stopped overdoing it several months into therapy because he was sick of being hung over. And sick of Dr. Denise instigating discussions about self-medication as a coping mechanism for trauma. When she challenged him to go *through* the pain instead of *around* it, he took the dare.

Leo always took a challenge, even if it hurt like hell.

Mel hurt worse. He loved their nightly cocktail hour, imbibing from his own glass by dipping his beak into it.

"Merlot."

"No, Mel, not tonight. Go dip into your water dish."

Squawk. "I want Merlot."

"Tough." Mel held out his hand, which Mel turned away from. "Mad at me?" Mel waddled over to the wine case and pecked at the cork in one of the bottles. "You missed your calling as a woodpecker, Mel." Leo popped open the cold soda, then told a long swig, savoring the cold lemony fizz.

"What's on the tube, Mel?" Leo strolled back into the living room, plunked down in the worn leather armchair which, besides several scattered TV trays, was the only furniture in the room. The chair creaked with Leo's weight. He picked up the remote control, punched a button, then watched the overly earnest TV newscaster talk about a Herbert-somebody who stole a camel from Circus Circus. Leo shook his head. "Herbert, you'd be better off stealing a car."

An image of Sandee and that Ferrari flashed through his mind. He'd congratulate her on her good taste, except she'd also stolen that Studebaker. Leo shook his head. "A Studebaker," he muttered. She'd probably already sold it on the black market—must have been a hungry buyer to want an ancient relic like a Studebaker, for God's sake.

But the Ferrari—now, that was different. A more interesting case for several reasons. First, how'd she steal it if the owner lived in Denver? And why didn't the owner press charges? Or was the owner, Tony Borgeson, here in town, spending the night in jail?

If so, why did Tony claim Sandee—or Corinne—was his fiancée?

Leo mulled over these facts, tumbling them like dice, coming up with different reasons. Had she been visiting Denver and talked this guy into marrying her, then stolen his car? She didn't seem that manipulative, but who was he to judge? He'd married Elizabeth. So however the car ended up in Vegas, why hadn't hotheaded Tony pressed charges, gotten the police involved? That was a hell of a lot easier than flying out here and causing a ruckus at the Grand.

The flutter of wings. Mel landed with a soft plop on the arm of the chair. He cocked his red and green head at Leo. "Hey, good-lookin'."

"You charmer, you." The woman's voice on the TV filled the background. He liked her honeyed tone, the way she tilted her head when she talked. Damn, it'd been a long time since he talked with a woman....

He watched the newscaster's red lips, the way they moved as she spoke, and he thought about Sandee's lips. Red, full. And that smile. Big, wholesome, sincere. Like Meg Ryan. He closed his eyes and tried to conjure Meg Ryan in a killer bikini, but instead he saw Sandee, sashaying around the ring, holding up cards as though there was nothing more important in the world, teasing an entire audience of men with her provocative walk, bright smile.

Squawk.

Leo looked at Mel. "Sorry, buddy. I'm not very good company tonight, am I? Won't drink with you, won't talk with you. I'm distracted. By a case."

Mel whistled a catcall.

"You're right. By a woman." He took another sip, staring down the parrot. "Okay, okay. I'll keep up my end of the conversation. She's got big gray eyes that can flash like silver or darken like storm clouds. A smile that could break your heart. A body that could bring the dead back to life. Her name's Sandee."

"Sandee."

Leo cocked an eyebrow. "You're quick."

"I want Sandee."

"That makes two of us." Damn, he shouldn't have said that. Now he couldn't think of anything else. He wanted her. Wanted to feel her, touch her, taste her. He'd been without a woman so long, the craving was damn near unbearable. He rolled the cold can between his hands, a futile antidote. Like throwing an ice cube at a bonfire. Nothing could quell his burning need. "Nothing but Sandee," he murmured.

Squawk. "I want Sandee."

"You're not helping." Leo got up and paced the hardwood floor. Everything he looked at was Sandee. The warm beige walls were her skin. The telecaster's red lips were Sandee's. And the overhead light fixture, with its white, round globes, were her...

Leo raked a hand through his hair. "I need a toothpick," he croaked. He headed for the kitchen, then remembered he'd left his pack in the car. Leo grabbed his keys. "Be right back, Mel."

But when he got to the car, he could care less about toothpicks. He fired the engine, telling himself he wanted to take a drive, clear his head.

Knowing what he really wanted was Sandee.

8

TWENTY MINUTES LATER, Leo parked across the street from Sandee's apartment, feeling mildly guilty that he'd lied to Mel. "It's his fault," Leo said to VD. "He started the 'I want Sandee' stuff, I didn't." VD hung, motionless, his round ball of a head staring at Leo. "Hey, I'm here because this is a job. I'm a detective, she's the suspect." Where were those toothpicks? Leo fumbled in the dark for the box, found it, and extracted one. Sometimes he missed smoking cigarettes so bad, he purposefully sat close to someone puffing away just so he'd get a whiff of secondhand smoke. But he'd made a commitment to the doctor, to himself, to be healthier. Popping the toothpick between his lips, he looked back at VD, who remained motionless, staring.

"Okay," Leo grumbled, "so I have the hots for Sandee. I'm human, something *you* wouldn't understand. But I got my priorities straight, I'm here to solve a crime, so don't you make me feel guilty, too." Jeez. Between Mel and VD, a guy could get a conscience.

Footsteps.

Leo darted his gaze around the area, caught a lone figure walking down the sidewalk. He turned up the walk to Sandee's apartment. Reaching her front door, he stepped into the yellow glare of her porch light.

"Thought you were locked up, bozo," Leo murmured, grabbing his cell phone. He'd call MGM Security, check status on Tony Borgeson, 'cause Leo was ninety-ninety percent certain that's who slugger was.

Leo started to punch in the number for information, then halted. If there were trouble, he didn't want to be distracted by a phone call.

"Sandee, open up!" The guy kicked the door. Leo shook his head at the testosterone tactics. "Yeah," he murmured, "there's gonna be trouble." Setting the phone on the seat next to him, he started to lift the door handle. No. If Sandee looked through her peephole and saw Leo *and* Tony on her doorstep, she'd blurt something about Tony sending Leo to her dressing room, then Tony would say he'd never seen Leo before in his life, and all hell would break loose.

Plan B. He grabbed the police radio and call for backup. He'd barely finished when the guy yelled again.

"Open up!" Thoroughly pissed, Tony paced in front of Sandee's door, then viciously kicked again.

Leo jumped out of the car as Tony's foot smashed against the door. To hell with waiting for the backups—Leo needed to protect Sandee. He'd wanted the backups so he wouldn't have to blow his cover, but if Sandee opened that door, Leo was going to be damn sure he was between her and Tony. Midway across the street, Leo heard Tony yell, "And who the hell are you?"

At first Leo thought Tony had seen him, which seemed impossible as this part of the street was in shadows. Then he saw Tony had spoken to the Brawny Baker, who'd appeared magically on the porch, his arms crossed across his massive chest, looking like a big bad Genie miffed he'd had to leave his bottle. Brawny said something, which Leo couldn't hear, but which must have been pretty damn good because Tony let loose with a wild swing.

Bad move.

Brawny calmly clutched the top of Tony's head, as though it were a basketball, and held him in place as Tony pounded the empty air between them.

Leo stepped onto the curb and shook his head. "What a waste of testosterone, Tony," he muttered.

A shriek.

Sandee had opened the door and was shrieking again as the flashing blue-and-red lights of two backup units pulsed the darkness. Leo pulled half a toothpick from his mouth, realizing he'd bit it in two when he'd heard her yell. He brushed the other half off his Hawaiian shirt, watching the buzz of activity on Sandee's porch. Officers heading to the porch. Flashlights. Handcuffs. Both men were escorted to different units, but only Tony was cuffed. One officer remained behind, scribbling notes in a book while Sandee, wearing a long pink T-shirt, talked.

Leo leaned against a parked car, a Volvo hidden in night shadow. Even if some of the cops recognized him, they knew he was undercover, so he was safe to simply watch and observe.

Specifically, observe Sandee. He liked that shirt. She'd worn it last night, too, when she'd been holding a spoon. A ring-card girl who wanted babies and cooked, too? Sexy and domestic? Why hadn't she settled down by now?

Ten minutes later, she stood alone on her porch, watching the last police unit drive off. Then she looked up at the stars, seemingly lost in thought. The porch light spilled yellow over her, casting her in a golden haze. With her face upturned, looking wistfully at the sky, she had an angelic look as though she were too pure, too fragile for this world.

Like hell.

"Face of an angel, body of a devil," Leo mumbled, repeating the words he'd heard in some country song. He glowered at her, suddenly furious at her for a hundred reasons. The Studebaker scam. Teasing men at the ring. Teasing *him...*

It didn't help that the T barely covered her thighs and exposed a pair of legs that made the term "hot legs" seem lukewarm. At the ring, she'd had security guards. At home, she had the Brawny Baker, who was heading toward some police station where he'd tell his version of the "disturbing the peace" scenario. *So, here she's alone, no guard, and what does she do? Hang out on her porch, seminaked, vulnerable to the next nut who has the hots for her.*

Which, as far as Leo knew, could be half of Vegas.

Feeling irrationally angry, Leo pushed off the car he leaned against and headed toward her, telling himself *he* wasn't the next nut. This was business. If she didn't have the sense to go back inside, he'd have to help her.

As he got close, her big gray eyes got bigger.

"It's you—"

"What're you doing staying outside, alone, after that crazy guy nearly kicked down your door?" Maybe he'd protected his cover before, but right now he was borderline blowing it and didn't give a damn.

"That crazy guy?" Narrowing her eyes, she fisted a hand on her hip. "Thought you knew Tony."

So Leo was right. It was Tony. "Get back in the house."

"I don't take orders."

Sexy, domestic and stubborn. "Please," he grumbled.

Her look softened, briefly, before turning angry again. "Why are you here?" Not waiting for a response, she jabbed an accusing finger at him. "You show up at my home. Show up in my dressing room..." She dropped the finger and instead nervously tugged on the end of the T-shirt, as though that might make it grow a few inches. A pink flush filled her cheeks.

He knew what she was thinking because he was thinking the same thing. He'd lost control in her dressing room, damn near attacked her. The only thing that didn't make him feel like a total jerk was she'd wanted it, too. He'd felt it in the way her body pressed against his, the way she returned his kiss...but still, he should never have let things go that far...

"I'm the one who called the cops tonight." Yeah, he sounded righteous, but it didn't quell the sting of what prompted him to come here in the first place.

"You knew Tony was headed over?" Her eyebrows pressed together in confusion.

"Yeah," he lied. It was a small lie. Enough to cover his tracks.

"You wanted to help me?"

Leo didn't like how that question sounded. As though she didn't believe it. He instantly hated the guy who'd made her feel insignificant. "Yeah." Another lie. Sort of. Leo had felt protective, which was in the line of duty...but his attraction to her was out of line.

God, he'd always lived life by his black-and-white rules. Right was right. Wrong was wrong. Yet here he was, straddling both moral absolutes. He was a detective covering his identity and, at the same time, a man hiding his desire. For the first time in his life, Leo stood in the gray, realizing what appeared to be wrong might also be right...

Her hoarse whisper broke the silence. "Thank you for calling the cops." She licked her lips nervously. "I didn't know what to do...." She sucked in a ragged breath and held it, as though holding back something she wanted to say.

"Do you want to talk?" For a moment, he felt like a jerk again because his question wasn't sincere. It was the detective kicking in, seizing the opportunity to ask her questions, get to the bottom of the bump-and-run scam. He reminded himself he had a job to do. And considering the mystery around the Denver-to-Vegas Ferrari, and the eyewitness who'd said Sandee was the redhead in the Studebaker bump and run, Leo couldn't lose this chance to dig, unearth some truth.

"Come inside," she said softly, heading toward her apartment.

Leo hesitated. Right or wrong to follow? He might be asking the questions, but he didn't have the answers anymore. His mind swirling with doubts, and anticipation, he fell into step behind her.

Corinne heard the door click shut, the sound resonating through her. It was like the jolts she'd experienced seeing Tony at the ring, hearing him on her doorstep. The latter had been particularly frightening as she watched the door shake with his kicks. Why hadn't her former fiancé just called? Asked for the car—wasn't that what he was after?

But she knew the answer as certainly as she stood here. Tony didn't view himself as the "former fiancé." In his mind, he was *still* her fiancé. Tony not only wanted the Ferrari back in his garage, he wanted his woman back in her place.

She turned to look at the guy who'd saved her skin tonight. The same skin now covered with small, skittering fires. He looked rough, unkempt, *manly*. The only guy in the world who could exude an edgy, sexual aura while wearing a Hawaiian shirt. "Can I get you something?" Forbidden thoughts of what she'd really like to give raced through her mind. "Iced tea, soda?" she whispered, as though that's what she'd been thinking.

He shook his head no. "So what's your relationship with Tony?"

Her stomach rippled with anxiety. He certainly cut to the chase. These past few days, Corinne had been too busy learning to be Sandee, the ring-card girl. She hadn't thought how "Sandee" might explain the relationship with Tony. Corinne waved her hand dismissively. "I wouldn't call it a relationship." *That* was for sure. Not anymore.

"Why'd he call you Corinne?"

Leo heard that? She hesitated, staring at an open-petaled pink flower on the shirt. She'd guessed before he didn't know Tony, but now she knew. Because if he'd known her former fiancé, he'd know who Corinne was. "You ask a lot of questions," she countered, meeting his gaze.

Maybe he was into playing a game, but she didn't

have the energy anymore. The last week's events suddenly weighed her down, wore her out. In a matter of days, she'd faced more than she had in her entire life. A weighty sigh escaped her lips.

"Sandee," he murmured huskily. He raised a hand as though to comfort her. "If you need a friend..."

"I do," she blurted, then pressed her lips together. Was she crazy, admitting that? But she did. She needed someone to unload to, turn to. Back home, she had Kyle. In Vegas, with her cousin gone, Corinne had nobody. This last week had been like one of those gravity-defying rides at an amusement park. She felt as though she'd been traveling at some insane speed, veering and careening to stay on course, and at this moment, she'd finally skidded to a mind-numbing stop.

But still there was no relief. It was as though she were holding on to the safety bar by her fingernails, trying to catch her breath, wanting to get off the ride but not knowing how...

"I'm here." His eyes sparked with tenderness.

For a dizzying moment, she almost let down her guard. But as much as part of her desperately wanted a friend, another part of her—the stoic, self-protective part—knew she had to keep her secret not only for herself, but for Sandee. Her cousin's employer thought Corinne was Sandee, the police thought Corinne was Sandee...she could create some serious problems for Sandee if she divulged what had really been going on these past few days.

She needed to keep the story straight. Keep up the façade for a few days more. Then Sandee would be back and they'd brainstorm what Corinne should do next.

Taking a deep, unsteady breath, she stepped back. "I'm okay," she lied. "It's late."

He searched her face as though trying to understand her shift in mood. "You're right," he said finally. "I should go." Then his green-eyed gaze dropped and a corner of his mouth kicked up in a lopsided grin. "What's that on your shirt?"

She looked down. Oh-h-h. She'd thrown on Sandee's Snow White and the Seven Dwarfs long T-shirt, but forgotten what it said on the front. I'm not Sleepy, are you? She closed her eyes, realizing how many people had probably read those words tonight. Tony. The Phantom. At least three cops. And now…Leo…

She opened her eyes. Leo's grin had settled into a more intimate smile. And in that instant, she remembered what it'd been like when his lips had taken hers. Hot, ferocious. And when his hands—roughened, strong—had caressed her. She opened her mouth to speak, but her voice refused to work. It didn't help that he continued to stare at the words, imprinted on the part of the shirt that covered her breasts. "It's— I'm—"

"I'm not sleepy, either," he said, his gaze returning to hers. His face, square and tan, gleamed in the lamplight. She noticed a white crescent-shaped scar above an eyebrow, which added a touch of brutality to his already rugged features. This wasn't a man who politely took, this was a man who devoured, consumed….

The tingling in her stomach flared to heat. The air felt thick, charged, just as it had in her dressing room.

She knew he felt it, too. His eyes glittered, like an animal's.

He shifted, moving imperceptibly closer. As though tracking her. Testing her. "Do you want me to leave?"

A shudder ripped along her spine. *No, don't leave.* Her body teetered on the threshold of wanting to experience the forbidden. And she wanted it so badly, she could taste its heat. Feel its tantalizing power. And all she had to do was say "No."

"Yes." The old Corinne had come to the forefront and spoken. The old Corinne who never buttoned past the second button, who never broke rules, who never asked for what she wanted.

His green eyes cooled. "I understand." He turned to leave.

"No," she whispered. But he was already opening the door, stepping outside. He tossed a look over his shoulder, a half smile that showed no mirth, then shut the door behind him.

She stood there, feeling gutted. She thought she'd changed in these last few days? No, she was still the old Corinne, denying what she wanted, doing what was "right." If she was going to be the old Corinne, she might as well go back to Tony, marry him, and lead a miserable life filled with games that were more hurtful and heartbreaking than any game she'd played in the last few days.

A shadow played across the decorative window next to the door. A faint snap snap snap. She remembered, that night in the parking lot, hearing this same sound. It'd been Leo, playing with the clasp on his watch. A nervous habit, she'd guessed at the time.

Snap snap snap.

So he was still outside, waiting. Watching her?

She flashed back on the scene at her doorstep in Denver. She'd been swathed in plastic wrap and high heels, wanting to entice the man she loved—thought she loved—because she was so desperate for his affection. Downright anxious to fuel his desire. But rather than feeling like a hot main course, she'd ending up feeling like plastic-wrapped leftovers.

I'm not leftovers. I deserve to feel wanted, desired.

I *want* to feel desired.

The new Corinne, the one who asked for what she wanted, surfaced. Boldly, she stepped toward the window. How much could he see? Probably shapes, forms...enough to know if she was standing, naked, wanting him. It was a risk Corinne had to take, now, or she'd forever step back into Never-Never Land.

Leo'd been watching her through this damn window that blurred everything into hazy shapes. He couldn't see the look on her face, but he could see she was still standing there, watching him. Why? She as much as told him to leave.

Mixed signals again. This lady was a puzzle, but after Elizabeth, he was an expert at games. He'd never again trust a woman after Elizabeth, even if the woman had sensitive gray eyes, danced with baby rattles and wore teasing little T-shirts.

He flinched, as though socked in the gut, when a truth hit him. *Judging all women by Elizabeth is just another way of viewing the world as black-and-white.* Just as Sandee's eyes were gray, so was the truth. Maybe something about her didn't feel right, but he'd know her story soon enough. The detective in him would ensure that.

Just as the man in him sensed her fundamental goodness. He'd seen that in the supermarket, when she'd danced in the baby aisle. He'd yet to meet a bad person who wanted to create life. Only goodness made people yearn for a child. He knew that from personal experience—maybe he'd done a lot of things wrong in his life, but wanting a child of his own had come straight from his heart. He also knew, after seeing her on the porch with Brawny Baker, that she treated others gently.

The man in him not only knew these things about her, but still sensed, in some gut-deep way, that they shared a connection. This time he wasn't scoffing at his gut instincts. He accepted it as part of the gray.

He played with his watch clasp, watching Sandee's hazy form through the glass pane. "You didn't want me to go, did you?" he whispered.

As though in response, the pink T-shirt moved up her body. She pulled it over her head, tossed it aside. Red strips crossed the blurred contours of pink skin. So she still had on that bikini. The mix of pink and red moved. Seemed to float back and forth. Was she walking in a circle? Like her act in the ring, except this show was for Leo only.

Heat seized him. He pressed one palm against the cool, slick glass and spread his fingers as though he could touch her.

The fleshy contours were indecipherable, like viewing a naked body under water. As his imagination filled in the missing definitions, a place in his belly went hard and hot. As he looked at the hazy shape through the glass, he remembered her pear-shaped breasts. Her nipples hardening under the weight of his gaze as though he'd touched her.

A strip of red floated off the pink—had she removed her top? When the second red strip dissolved in a puddle at her feet, he released a pent-up growl. She moved closer, revealing her nakedness. Through the whorls of patterned glass, he caught flashes of dark pink nipples. Teasingly red hair between thighs.

His engorged desire demanded release. He grabbed the handle of the door. Locked. Had to get in. Had to get to her. He paced, back and forth, his senses painfully acute. The fragrance of jasmine assaulted his nose. The overhead light burned his skin. He wouldn't be sane, be whole until he had her.

Had to get to her.

He grabbed the door knob again and shook it, hard. The door shuddered. With a fierce growl, he shoved his weight, shoulder first, against the door. A cracking sound, like the world ripping, and the door flew open.

Heat exploded in Corinne's chest as she jumped back. Her heartbeat skyrocketed as the door slammed against the wall. Leo stood, looking at her as he had in the dressing room. Like an animal unleashed.

She knew if she said "no," he'd stop. But that was the last thing she wanted. She'd been rejected on a doorstep before, not again. "Take me," she whispered, her voice barely audible.

For a split second, her resolve wavered. *Have I lost my mind? I hardly know the man.*

But she did. When he'd walked in on her naked that first night, he could have taken advantage of her. He didn't. And tonight, he could have let Tony harm her.

He didn't. No, she knew this man. She knew Leo. Just as, for the first time in her life, she knew her sexuality, her power as a woman.

"Take me," she repeated, her voice stronger.

9

HE CLOSED THE DOOR, his glistening green eyes promising all the lusty, forbidden things Corinne had ever dreamed about. And when he tore off his shirt, her heart thumped wildly against her chest.

She closed her eyes, waiting for the inevitable. Any moment he was going to sweep her away and make mad, wild, out-of-control-come-take-me-now-now-*now* love to her. She tightened her knees, not wanting to crumble at the first impact of hot, wild male. And it would be an impact—one doozy of one—because he'd undoubtedly propel his body across the room the way he propelled his body against the door. One ferocious, libido-driven rush of woman-hungry movement. God, her insides were trembling, as though they might rip apart any moment, just like the door. *I teased, now you take.* She licked her lips, waiting...

Nothing happened.

She opened one eye.

He just stood there!

She rolled back her shoulders, as though that helped her see better. To be absolutely correct, he wasn't *just* standing there, he was...sort of...crouched there. His entire body was tensed, as though he were prepared to pounce. And he was breathing, hard, as if he'd run a great distance to get to her. With each intake of nostril-flaring air, his chest swelled, showing off pecs carpeted with dark hair that swept wildly across his torso.

She eased out a shaky breath. That rendezvous in her dressing room with Leo was simply a spicy appetizer to the fiery feast that stood before her now. This hunk of masculinity was more than Tony could ever dream to be, more man than she'd ever dreamed of…

And what a man.

Leo's presence dominated the room, churning the air with his scent, his heat. Her gaze traveled down his chest, following the trail of chest hair that narrowed to a V at the waistband of his jeans. The old Corinne would have stopped there.

Not the new.

Her gaze traveled down his jeans, over those bulging thighs and that wide-legged stance, over the threadbare area around his manhood, up to…

Threadbare?

Her eyes shifted back down to his crotch. What kind of man wore out the denim over *that* part? Her heartbeat escalated from wild thumping to erratic pounding. She'd only been with one man, Tony, and none of his pants wore out at that spot. Not even *one* thread. Plus denim was a rugged, durable material. The stuff cowboys wore. Only something big, that pushed hard against that tough fabric, could make it *threadbare.*

He's like an animal.

Leo shifted, his movement distracting her threadbare inventory. She looked up.

He stepped purposefully, slowly toward her, as though stalking his prey. The corners of his mouth curved dangerously down as a low growl reverberated from deep in his throat. A wild thrill coursed through her.

He *is* an animal.

Before his presence churned the air. Now it electrified it. Her entire body felt the charged connection. What was he waiting for? A signal? She'd already told him to take her. Criminey, she stood here, *naked*. What more could he want? How did the female animal signal her readiness to the male? Instinctively, Corinne slid one bare foot to the side, opening herself, silently giving him permission.

Just like that crashing door, the room exploded.

In a rush of movement, he lunged as she moved forward. They collided somewhere in the middle of the room, entangled in each other's arms, their lips frantically searching each others. "Leo, Leo," she murmured between breaths, crazy with need for him. The need heightened by her gut-level knowledge that at this moment, Leo held *her, Corinne,* not her fabrication of Sandee. The world fell away, replaced by sensations. His mouth plundering hers. Fingers tunneling her hair. The fierce ache in her gut. And in the midst of the frenetic kissing, touching, caressing, some distant corner of her mind tried to capture this moment, burn it forever into her memory, so she'd always remember what it felt like to be the sole object of a man's desire.

When he pulled back to catch a breath, she looked into his eyes, hot and filled with admiration, and felt more womanly than she ever had in her life. And when his hand slid down her torso, searing a burning path, and dipped teasingly into the crevice between her legs, she rose onto her tiptoes. "O-h-h-h, ye-e-es!"

Then Corinne grabbed his head with her hands,

yanked him to her, and damn near devoured the man with a frenzied kiss. She thought he was making more of those guttural sounds, then realized it was her. She also realized her left leg was wrapped tightly around his thigh, effectively pinning him to her.

Hello, New Corinne! She tugged her leg tighter, molding him against her, as her lips continued to kiss, suck, nibble his mouth. And she'd thought him to be an animal? Right now, she ruled the jungle.

Air. She needed air. Pulling back, she gasped a lungful, then dove for his chest where she resumed her kissing and licking, relishing the coarse texture of his hair, the salty taste of his skin. Then she rubbed her face against that hairy mat, drenching herself in his masculine scent.

He said something unintelligible.

She looked up, meant to say "What?" But when she opened her mouth, all that came out was a breathy, mewing sound. She wasn't sure if he looked surprised or confused. She didn't care. There was so much man, so little time.

Her hands began stroking and fondling his muscled torso. Her fingers explored and caressed hard curves and indentations, stopping momentarily on a raised scar on his chest before skimming that V of hair down to the waistband...*there*...her fingers brushed that threadbare spot.

He sucked in an appreciative breath.

She wrapped her fingers around the hardened bulge, gently massaging that threadbare denim.

He emitted a low, needy moan.

Oh boy. She fumbled with the button on his jeans. Time to...

"Honey, not yet," he murmured. Slowly, he took both her hands in his and held them tightly. "I don't want to take you here..."

She nodded, although she didn't care if he took her in the middle of Highway 10. "The bedroom..." She started to head toward the hallway when a strong hand grabbed her arm.

"With me," he whispered urgently. "After I shut the door...fortunately the chain still works..."

And then he was back, sweeping her into his arms, cradling her in his embrace. She seemed surprised, then delighted. Curling up her legs, she leaned her head on his shoulder and pointed toward the hallway. "That way," she said softly.

Leo carried her toward the room, thinking how soft she felt, how suddenly fragile, huddled in his arms naked like this. He'd damn near lost it on the porch, breaking the door, then lunging across the room for her. But after a year of being out of control with experiences blurring and slamming into each other, he wanted to take this sizzling, sweet moment and stretch it out, make it last.

He headed down the single hallway. One door led to the bathroom, the other to her bedroom. He walked toward the latter and stopped inside. It looked like a decorated peach. Orange colored walls, bedspread, curtains. White wicker dressing table and matching dresser drawers with little peach-colored knobs. *Doesn't seem her style.* But the thought disappeared as his gaze shifted to the bed.

He walked over, gently lowered her, then stepped back to admire the view. He'd seen her naked on several occasions—in her dressing room, through that pane of glass, but he'd never taken the time to savor her feminine beauty. Lying on top of that orange bedspread, her flesh glowed. Tonight it wasn't just a lovely pink, as he'd observed that first night in her dressing room. Tonight it glowed from within, giving it an almost luminescent sheen. His gaze wandered over her, slowly. She looked like a painting, one of those lush numbers that depicted a beautiful woman reclining on a sofa, her hair spilling around her face, wearing nothing but a smile.

"God, you're beautiful."

Her eyes moistened and for a moment, he thought she'd cry. But she didn't. Instead, she smiled a thank-you, an act so sweet and appreciative, that he suddenly saw through her nakedness, straight down to her soul, to a truth that bordered on painful.

She's never been made love to.

Had sex, yes, but never experienced the touch of a man who cherished her. The realization bubbled up from a place beyond logic, from that place where before he'd sensed their connection. That gray area, where black and white didn't matter. Because at this moment, it didn't matter what she might have done in the past or dreamed of in the future. All that mattered was here and now. And that he was about to make love to a beautiful woman whose desire for him was the most treasured gift he'd ever been offered.

He reached for the lamp on the dresser. "Let's turn this off," he said huskily. With a click, the room shifted to shadows. Stray light spilled from the hallway into the room, across the bed, highlighting the delicious contours of her body. "Nice," he murmured.

He slowly undid the button at his waistband,

watching her watching him. He pulled off his socks and shoes. Then he let the zipper down slowly, removed his pants, and stood naked in front of her. She watched with such innocent fascination, he nearly smiled. The light from the hallway hit his back, so the front of his body was effectively in shadow, but he figured she saw enough to know what she was in for.

"Nice," she whispered.

"Copycat."

She giggled at their shared joke. He liked the sound. Girlish, happy.

But when she rolled over onto her side, one mischievous eye peeking through her tousled hair, she didn't look girlish anymore. She was a woman. Sexual, primed. And when she crooked one finger in a come-here gesture, he had to hold himself back from throwing himself at her.

With tremendous self-control, he lowered himself next to her on the bed and took her hand, caressing it with his lips. It was a small hand, delicate like a flower. He kissed her arm, her shoulder, her neck. She moved languorously, her breaths catching. When, finally, he grazed his lips along her earlobe and released a warm breath, she gasped. Goose bumps skittered across her skin.

Hot need knifed through him, but still he held back.

Propping himself onto one elbow, he leaned toward her, drinking in her lovely face. Her eyes were half-closed, their look dreamy and desirous. He pulled a wayward hair off her cheek, then let his finger play along her jaw, her chin, before slowly outlining the fullness of her lips.

"Kiss me," she whispered.

"Ordering me around, again?" he murmured, touching the corner of her mouth.

"Yes," she admitted, smiling.

"Your wish is my command." He lowered his head and kissed her soft mouth.

But it was more than a kiss. It was as though his soul melted into hers. Pleasure radiated through him, rousing his passion. God, he wanted to take it slow. With a groan, he trailed a hand across her smooth belly to her breasts. He cupped their fullness and squeezed, fighting another surge of heat as her breaths quickened. After drawing teasing circles around a nipple, he trapped it between his thumb and index finger and tugged the puckered tip.

She writhed, her hands roaming restlessly over his shoulders, his back. And when he suckled on her breast, she whimpered, "Oh yes, more, more..."

He lifted his head. "Still ordering me around?"

She blinked. "Isn't my...wish...your command?"

"Yes," he said suggestively, "but more what?" He massaged her nipple, then eased his weight on top of her and rubbed his bare chest against her breasts, savoring the way their tight buds thrust against him. He positioned a leg between hers and forced them open wider. Then he moved his thigh against the delta and gently pressed.

"More...there," she said breathlessly.

He trailed a hand down her upper body and parted the soft, wet crease. "There?"

"Almost."

He shifted his hand.

"Oh-h-h ye-e-s." She arched her back and groaned as he increased the rhythm.

The heat in his groin was damn near unbearable, but he held back, wanting to watch her pleasure. But when she lifted her hips and said in that breathy, begging voice, "Please take me...now...please..." her wish was his command.

"Do you have...? He kept massaging, not wanting to break the momentum.

She turned her head to look at him. "Have?"

"Protection."

Her eyes, feverish, stared at him, then she frowned. "Thought I saw some..." She lifted a lazy finger and pointed at the nightstand. "...in there."

He looked at the wicker stand and its one drawer, then back to his hand still massaging her soft furrow. "Hate to leave you at a time like this...think you could get one?"

"Oh, right." Without moving her body even a millimeter, she flung her arm over the side of the bed, tugged on the drawer handle, and fumbled through the contents.

He had no doubt this was one of those women who could also put on makeup while careening down the freeway at eighty miles an hour.

"Oh-h-h!"

He slowed his hand's movement. "Did you—?"

"Yes!" She waved a small foil packet. "I found it!"

He smiled. Honest to God, he'd never been with a woman who so honestly revealed her desires. To know that a woman wanted you like this was a powerful aphrodisiac. "Open it." Not moving his fingers off her nub, he shifted onto his knees. His body gleamed in the light from the hallway.

Her eyes opened wide. "No wonder they're threadbare!"

"Wha—?" But he lost the thought as she slipped the sheath over his hardness. Her touch was silky, yet firm. When she'd finished, he positioned himself over her and gently eased the tip of his shaft between her legs. She raised her knees, guiding him with her hand. He sank into her. When she gasped with pleasure, the fire he'd been holding back flamed higher.

And higher.

He cupped the lush roundness of her butt and moved, his hips executing long, sliding thrusts. His blood boiled, his heart thundered. But he held himself in check with measured strokes, not wanting to rush...wanting this to be good for her. He squeezed shut his eyes, felt the sweat on his forehead.

Soft hands wiped his brow.

He looked down.

Her gray eyes glistened, their color like silver. Within those depths, he caught the glint of lust that mirrored his own. Then she arched her back, her lips quivering. He picked up speed, stroking harder, harder...

She yelled his name, her body pulsing. Heat erupted, bursting through him as a long, harsh groan escaped his lips. And in that moment of suspended ecstasy, his entire being felt their physical, and soul-deep, connection.

His weight on his elbows, he held himself over her before collapsing onto her body. "Am I hurting you?" he whispered, ready to move.

She wrapped her arms around him. "Are you kidding?" She nuzzled his neck. "I feel...the best I have...in my entire life."

Closing his eyes, he inhaled her rose scent. So did he.

"WELL, IF IT ISN'T Red's boyfriend, again." The squat security guard glanced at the dozen red roses Leo was holding. "Good move. The other one didn't bring a gift."

"Other one?"

"The guy who got here before you."

Tony was back? Leo had already figured that last night, when Tony had tried to enter at this back entrance, he'd wanted to find Sandee's dressing room. When he didn't, he'd wandered about the boxing ring until she showed up. But tonight, undoubtedly not wanting to chance another public confrontation, Tony had probably talked his way in—with a neatly creased twenty—and was looking for her dressing room, ready to harass her about that damn car.

Conflicting emotions rose within Leo. Last night, after he and Sandee had made love, Leo didn't wanted to play detective. He just wanted to be a man, to hold the woman who'd broken through his shield, who'd made him feel whole, alive again. Because of a morning meeting with Dom, Leo had to leave her place early. Before kissing her goodbye, he'd called a contractor pal who promised to fix the door that morning.

Then Leo had spent the rest of the day taking care of business, although his thoughts kept returning to Sandee. Before he'd left, she sleepily said she wanted to talk to Leo, something they hadn't had time to do the night before. He'd agreed, thinking he wanted to ask about her nightly visitors.

Like Tony, who had shown up tonight, again.

Squatty pulled a pack of cigarettes out of his shirt pocket. "Yeah, Hank's back."

Hank? Leo's thoughts did a three-sixty. So Hank was tonight's surprise visitor? Leo didn't exactly like Squatty, but this guy was becoming the closest thing to a buddy Leo had. "Hank's a good guy," Leo lied, not having a clue. "They're just friends now..." He let it hang, waiting for Squatty to verify Leo's assumption.

"If you say." Squatty tapped a cigarette loose from the box.

Hardly the verification Leo was looking for. Plus, this guy's gossipy, know-it-all attitude pissed Leo off. He stepped closer. So close, he saw the little red veins in Squatty's nose. "I say."

"Hotheaded, huh?" Squatty squinted one eye, sizing up Leo. "Just like the rest of her guys. That Sandee fuels more passion in men than an energy company."

If Leo hadn't been holding the roses, he'd have thrown a left hook. "Your nose must get sore, sticking it all the time into other people's business."

Squatty edged back a step. "Hey," he mumbled. "I was just kiddin'."

"Too bad you can't get a job in comedy," Leo muttered, stepping inside. He entered the backstage area, welcoming the rush of air-conditioning. Maybe it would cool his temper before he got to Sandee's dressing room.

He headed down the familiar dark hallway. *Everybody has her wrong.* He knew it in his gut, and he'd prove it. There were a zillion redheads in the world, at least two million in Vegas alone, so he'd have to pick up the scent of one of them because there was no way this Sandee could be a con.

Plus, Leo had been around long enough to know that whatever was going on with Tony Borgeson and his Ferrari, it wasn't a case of theft. Besides, Tony had earned the Mr. Whacked Out award when he'd shown up here at the Grand, bullied Sandee, called her the wrong name—Corinne—and the grand finale, slugged a security guard.

Too bad it wasn't Squatty he'd slugged, Leo thought with a grin.

Heading down the second hallway, Leo quickened his pace. He felt anxious, excited to see Sandee. Like a kid courting his first girl.

Her dressing room door was cracked open. Leo almost pushed it open when he heard a man's voice.

"Baby, I know I was wrong. I admit it. But after losing my job, I'm havin' problems making ends meet. I need just one more bump and run to get me over the edge."

Through the cracked door, Leo saw flashes of a guy's dark curly hair and a pec T-shirt. *So that's Hank. Talking about a bump and run?* Leo's gut tightened, waiting for Sandee's response. Just because this Latin ex-lover mentioned that kind of car scam, didn't mean Sandee knew about it...didn't mean she was guilty...

"I can't—" she said softly.

Leo squeezed shut his eyes. That wasn't incriminating, a simple "I can't."

"Hank, I can't do that again with you."

Damn it. Do it *again?* She was admitting to having been an accomplice in a crime.

Just as Leo thought the words, Hank slammed his fist on the counter top. "It's not like I'm asking for the world! You did it once, you can do it again. Then I'll never, never ask for a favor like this. I promise."

"Never, never," she murmured. "No, I can't. And that's final."

It was like being shot all over again. Blasted, point blank, by the ugly truth. So Sandee was nothing but a common, lying criminal. Leo looked at the roses, their sweet scent almost sickening him. *I've trusted another con. Given my heart to another woman who lives a lie.*

He turned, stormed back the way he'd come, tossing the roses into the first trash can he passed. Just the way he was tossing Sandee out of his mind, out of his heart.

THIRTY MINUTES LATER, Leo stared at his Airstream trailer. Its polished silver shell sparkled under the streetlamp's light. He took a swig of his soda, let it fizz on his tongue, then swallowed, slowly. He really wanted a beer. Or five or six. But this past year he'd learned, the hard way, how self-medicating didn't fix pain.

"So instead I'm standing in my front yard," he grumbled, "consoling myself with a lemon-lime soda." He downed the rest of the drink, crushed the can with his fist and tossed it into the trash bin.

The can hit the pavement with a tinny thwack and clattered to a stop. "Missed the trash. Missed the clues about Sandee. I'm on a roll."

So much for "the Wolf is back," he thought, heading

over to the soda can. He'd been hot on the trail, primed for the kill...then he'd let his heart take the driver's seat and steer him in the wrong direction. He picked up the can. Standing over the trash container, he dropped it in.

Heading back up the driveway, he stopped again to look at his Airstream. Fondly called the "Silver Bullet" by Airstream lovers. He snorted a derisive laugh. "Silver Bullet, that's a good one. Wasn't that what killed the Wolfman?"

Tracking Sandee had pretty much done the same to the Wolf.

Because he no longer cared. That thirst to regain his detective status, to excel on the force, was dead. Prior to the shooting, he'd loved being "the Wolf," the biggest, baddest Sin City detective. Loved the reputation, the way he got respect from his peers and supervisors. But that was when his life had seemed perfect. When he'd had a home, a wife, a future...

Then a twist of fate had turned all that upside down. And after a year of recovery, he was fighting to reclaim who he was...

"I've been fighting for the wrong thing," he suddenly said. "I should fight for what I want, not what the world expects of me."

Not a small coincidence he reached this realization standing in his yard, staring at the Silver Bullet. He'd bought it on a whim, for a mere grand, several months after he'd been shot. He'd figured it was a crazy idea, buying an old trailer that needed more fixing up than he did. He'd laughed about it when he'd told his therapist, but Dr. Denise had just given him that quiet, wise stare, as though seeing more into his words than he did.

And after that, when his rage flared or he couldn't sleep, he'd go outside and take out his frustrations on this trailer. He'd sweat and toil and curse until he exhausted himself. But now he had a renovated Airstream, the result of his hard work.

He remembered Dr. Denise saying one day he'd also see a new Leo Wolfman—also the result of his hard work.

He didn't need to hold up a mirror to see the new Leo Wolfman tonight. "I'm tired of prowling the seedy side of Vegas," he admitted. "I want a new life, the life I've dreamed about." He cocked his head and stared down the Silver Bullet. "The life I dreamed about as I remodeled you."

How many times, while polishing the outside shell, or installing some new gadget inside, had Leo daydreamed about that small ranch. Figured it would take two more years on the force, saving money, to get the down payment. Well, he was ready to stop dreaming and start doing. What did he have to lose? His mom and stepdad had retired to the mountains of New Mexico. Elizabeth was gone with everything he once owned. All Leo had was Mel, VD, an old Mustang and the Silver Bullet. Wouldn't be difficult to transplant them. *If I can hang in there for a few more years on the force, I can make my dream real.*

He began rolling up his sleeves. It was fitting that the last piece of remodeling he needed to finish his Airstream was to put up those custom curtains that had arrived last week. He'd install them tonight, but leave them open. Then every time he walked by his trailer, he'd imagine one day being inside the Silver Bullet and looking out at a new landscape.

A new landscape on a small ranch he could call his own.

"G'NIGHT, HONEY," the security guard said with a wink. "Save some o' that sweet stuff for me."

This guy was getting on Corinne's nerves. Every time she came in, every time she left, he said the same ol' chauvinistic thing. She pivoted and gave him a searing look. "I don't mind you calling me 'honey.' I figure it's part of this job. But please don't refer again to my 'stuff.' It's my body. *My* body. And I'd like it to be respected *please*."

Wow. Even Corinne was shocked at her little speech. Inconspicuous Corinne had become conspicuous not only physically, but verbally as well.

The guard seemed shocked at her little speech, too. His mouth dropped open and hung there for a moment. Then he muttered, "Sorry."

"Thank you." She turned and headed toward the parking lot, feeling stronger for that exchange. The warm breezes ruffled her hair as she veered right after a bunch of palms. She'd started using this landmark so she'd easily find the Ferrari after work—otherwise, she'd get lost in this huge parking lot. *Right at the palms, then five cars down...*

Funny. She stopped and looked around at the sea of vehicles. She was certain she'd parked it here. She walked through a line of cars, surveyed the area, then retraced her steps. No, she was dead certain she'd parked here, she even remembered this funky yellow Volkswagon parked next to her because it had such a cute license plate. NEVRL8. *Never Late*. Ha, the way she used to be!

She stared at the license plate, then at the car parked next to it, a four-door economy number. Where the Ferrari had been parked three hours ago...

Tony. He took his car.

She felt a flutter of anxiety, but it blew away like one of these desert breezes. The Ferrari's disappearance was another piece of her old life gone. Just as the old Corinne was going, going, almost gone. She just wished she knew who the new Corinne was becoming. She'd think about that later—right now, she'd grab a cab home. Rent a car tomorrow.

Her only concern was that Tony still wanted the car *and* her. Not because she was his ideal partner, but because that's what his family expected of him and he'd live up to the tradition, so help him God. In his deranged sense of being the good Italian son, he undoubtedly thought he'd still marry good Corinne and she'd be a good wife.

"Never, never, never," she whispered. Returning to her old life, Never-Never Land, was *not* an option.

She headed back to the Grand. As she approached the guard, she saw Hank standing there, arguing. Before the boxing match, she'd told him to go, that she wasn't bumping and running with him anymore, whatever *that* meant. He'd been emotional, which seemed to be his usual state, but he'd left. And now he was back. Stubborn, wasn't he.

As the click click click sound of her heels got closer, Hank turned, looking immensely relieved when he saw her. *"Mi amante—"*

"What're you doing back here?"

Hank's big brown eyes turned sentimentally moist. He pulled a rose out from behind his back. The guard raised his eyebrows, but said nothing. "I came back to apologize." He handed her the rose. "I was wrong, Sandee. I'm sorry."

If she didn't accept this rose and apology, God knows what the passionate Hank would do next. She had no doubt he'd drop to his knees right here, on the asphalt, and start that "I'd climb the highest mountain" speech again.

She accepted the rose. "Thank you."

"Can I buy you dinner, baby? You're looking a little thinner lately."

Maybe she didn't need to call a cab after all. "Rain check? But, uh, I could use a lift home." She'd figure out how to sidestep the bumping and running later. Anyway, Hank was so determined to get back into Sandee's good graces, he probably wouldn't be pushing for that soon again.

Hank's eyes lit up. "Anything for my baby." He put his hand on her back and eased her in the direction of his car.

As Corinne exited with Hank, she heard the guard say quite professionally, "G'night, Ms. Moray."

"Look at her, VD," Leo said, chomping on a toothpick. "And carrying a rose, too." How could she make love to him last night, then be leaving with this guy tonight? *Because he's her partner in crime. Part of their scam.*

Which only fueled Leo's justification that he'd returned here. After working on his Silver Bullet, he'd been too worked up to call it a night. Figured he might as well wrap up this case. After all, he needed a few more years on the force to save money...might as well prove himself, show he knew how to be a detective again. That or spend the next forty-eight months chained to a desk.

The Tracker lurched out of the lot. Either that guy didn't know how to drive, or it was yet another stolen vehicle he wasn't comfortable driving. Man, this was becoming one of the screwiest cases Leo'd ever handled. Bungling, passionate thieves. Sexy, innocent women.

If Leo wasn't so busy grinding his teeth on this toothpick, he might laugh.

Thirty minutes later, Leo had tailed them to the outskirts of Vegas. Where were they headed? This was definitely away from Sandee's apartment. Great. Like Leo wanted to follow her and some date back to his place. Wouldn't that be the finishing jolt to a rollercoaster day.

"Dom should've kept me at that desk. Days into my first detective gig and I'm tailing a woman I've fallen for while she's on a date with another guy." Okay, he'd confessed it. Despite everything, he'd fallen for her. For the woman who flashed sex and sweet in the blink of an eye. The woman who could prance hot around a ring and dance gently with a baby rattle.

He licked his lips. The woman who'd kissed him like she meant it. Who'd whispered his name in his ear as though he were the most important man in the world.

His stomach clenched remembering last night, remembering her stoked passion. *I need to chill.* He rolled down his window. But instead of sobering, blasting air, warm desert breezes trailed into the car. The sweetened air conjured memories of her scent. The ruffling breezes were like her fingers burrowing through his hair.

Damn her, anyway. Just when he'd thought he'd gotten his act together, a woman was tearing him apart.

Screeeeech!

The Tracker slammed on its brakes. The stench of rubber filled the air. VD swung wildly as Leo pumped the brakes. Ahead, the vehicle swiveled to the right, kicking up clouds of dirt as it rode the shoulder.

Then it careened off the road and disappeared from view.

10

LEO JERKED THE WHEEL of his Mustang and pulled off the road. Jumping out of the car, he cursed himself for not thinking better, smarter. He shouldn't have let Sandee leave the Grand with Hank, shouldn't have let them drive to this desolate highway. What the hell were they doing? Didn't matter. *Nothing* mattered, except to know she was okay.

Leo jogged to the edge of the road and looked down to where the Tracker disappeared. From what he could discern in the moonlight, the ground dropped off sharply for a few feet, then sloped another ten or so. A little beyond that sat the Tracker, tilted at an angle, its headlights beaming on a gnarled cactus. Leo's body went cold with apprehension. *God, let her be okay.* He tore down the incline, his feet sliding over dirt and scattered rocks.

Reaching level ground, he jogged to the passenger side, whose door hung ajar. Had she been thrown? Panic assaulted him. He scanned the area. Every shape and shadow could be her crumpled body, lying in a lifeless heap.

"Why'd you grab the wheel?" barked a man's voice. "Now look at the mess we're in."

"You almost rear-ended that car!" snapped Sandee. "I saved our lives!"

Leo jerked his gaze back to the Tracker, the source

of the squabbling. He blew out a gust of air. So far, so good. They were inside the vehicle. No thrown bodies. And angry yelling meant a good chance no one was hurt. He took a step toward the Tracker when a furious Sandee leaped out. Simultaneously, the driver's door flew open—or tried to. It thunked hard against something. More cursing. Out hopped Hank.

"Great! I just dented the door on a cactus!" Hank slammed his fist on the hood.

"And dented the car with your fist," retorted Sandee. "Blaming me for that, too?"

Leo started to ask if there were any injuries, but it would have meant yelling louder than these yellers, which at the moment seemed an impossible task. Although the moonlight glazed over shapes and forms, it was dark out here. Dark enough that they hadn't noticed Leo yet.

But then, it could be high noon, and these two probably wouldn't notice anyone outside of their heated exchange.

"Saved our lives…" Hank muttered, obviously not wanting to stay on the dent topic. He raised his voice. "You call grabbing a steering wheel, jerking it one-eighty and crashing it into a ditch 'saving lives'?" He snorted loudly.

"You call colliding with another vehicle a precautionary driving practice?"

"Precautionary?" Hank paused. "Since when did you start using such big words?"

"Since I went on this joyride with you!"

As Hank griped and muttered—reminding Leo of an oversized Mel—Sandee headed around the front of the car and marched through the angled beams. In that flash of light, she certainly looked unhurt. In fact, she looked damn near ferocious, in a feminine sort of way. Leo thought he'd seen all her attitudes, but this was a new one. With her jutting chin, pumping arms, and long strides, she looked like a Victoria's Secret model training for a triathlon.

She began scrambling up the incline. Or Leo presumed she was scrambling. From the scraping, sliding sounds intermixed with some very impressive cuss words, she certainly seemed determined to make it up that incline. Although why she'd blind herself in the headlights, then charge up a dark slope confounded him.

She needs help. Leo took off after her. He still didn't know if these people were okay. Physically, anyway. Then he saw her silhouette at the top of the embankment. Her body carved a sensuous line against the star-splattered desert sky. All lean with fullness in the right places. His gut knotted up as memories of their lovemaking blasted through him.

She teetered for balance. Waving her hands madly, she shrieked and began to fall backward.

Leo shot forward, Hank close behind.

They raced up the embankment, Leo catching what felt like a shoulder. Hank seemed to grab her legs. The men fought for balance as they slid back down, miraculously carrying their squirming, yelping cargo without dropping her. Reaching level ground they set her on her feet.

Leo heaved several deep breaths, wondering if *that* surge of adrenalin would ever subside. "Anybody hurt?" he finally asked.

"Who...are...you?" gasped Hank, leaning over, his hands on his knees.

A shriek.

Leo and Hank both started. Leo looked around. Now what was she trying to crawl?

"You—you!" Sandee said from where they'd deposited her.

Good. She was staying put. Leo needed a breather before another bout of crawling, grabbing, and carrying. "Yes, it's me," he answered matter of factly.

"What are you doing here?"

"Rescuing you, it appears." Leo swiped the sweat off his brow. "Anybody hurt?"

Both muttered "no."

"Good." Leo looked at the lopsided Tracker. "The three of us can't do anything with your vehicle tonight. Best to leave it here. Hank, why don't you get the keys, turn off the lights. I'll call a tow truck." He headed back to his Mustang.

"How'd you know my name's Hank?"

"Lucky guess." *Two more years and that ranch is mine.*

A few minutes later, Leo stood outside his car, talking on his cell phone to a towing service. When Sandee appeared over the top of the ditch, alone, he felt a stab of guilt. He figured she'd wait for Hank, and they'd scramble to the top together, hand in hand.

He should have waited, helped her.

And she should have told the truth. About Hank, about the bump and run, about what last night meant.

A muscle twitched in his jaw. Screw the guilt. He tried to ignore her as he wrapped up his conversation, but she stood in the headlights of his Mustang, making it about as easy to ignore her as ignore a billboard.

A very sexy billboard. The lights revealed the translucence of her top and the little teddy she wore underneath. And those jeans, which looked sprayed on, were a poor excuse for clothing. It was amazing she'd been able to scramble in those things. Even more amazing she was able to breathe.

Leo turned away. He'd just gotten hot images of her out of his head, and now she was burning them back in again. He ended the conversation and got in his car, flicking the headlights off.

Several minutes later, Sandee was in the front seat, Hank in the back. Her rose scent invaded his car space, another lethal reminder of last night when her scent teased and tormented him.

Like it was doing now.

"Put your seat belts on," Leo ordered gruffly.

Sandee did a double take. "You can ask nicely."

Wasn't that like a woman. They take a knife to your heart, then wonder why you're bleeding. "Put your seat belts on, *please.*"

"Baby," Hank murmured, leaning forward over the seat, "the man's helping us out."

"Yeah." chimed in Leo. "And in case you're not certain *which* man is helping you out, it's *this* man." Okay, even he wasn't sure what that meant, but he felt the urge to say *something* on his behalf. Besides, if the saying "the best man wins" was true, Leo was the best one for this lady whether she knew it or not.

"That's right," added Hank. "He's the man. Do as he says, baby."

Corinne exploded. "If one more *man* corrects me, calls me 'baby,' or tells me what to do, so help me I'll get out of this car and walk all the way back to Vegas."

She jerked tight the seat belt and snapped it loudly into place. Which was the last sound made in the car during the long, tense ride home.

WHEN THEY HIT THE south side of town, Leo said sullenly, "Who wants to be dropped off first?"

Hank, sounded gratingly cheery, said, "Just take us to Sandee's—"

"No." Maybe Corinne was pretending to be Sandee, but that act didn't extend into Sandee's bedroom, where she had no doubt Hank thought they'd end up. And besides, that bedroom was sacred ground after last night, although you'd never know it from the way Leo was acting. Virtually ignoring her at the accident. Barking at her to put on her seat belt. And on the way home, sneaking sideways glances as though she might do something weird. Like what, she wondered. Grab the steering wheel? Steal that strange feathery thing that dangled from his rearview mirror?

Plus, she felt miffed that he'd followed her tonight like some kind of stalker. Okay, she was grateful he'd rescued them, and thrilled when she'd first realized he was there, but that was because he'd been *tailing* her. Didn't he trust her? And his smug, "I'm the man" attitude was obviously a macho-overload reaction because he thought she was two-timing him.

Being Sandee was becoming a problem. At first, it had been invigorating, thrilling. But now she was growing a bit anxious for Sandee to return so Corinne could figure who *she* was...and the longer she masqueraded as Sandee, the longer it would be before she discovered the new Corinne. For the first time, a fear took hold—what if she didn't learn from this experience? What if she never fully evolved, became someone new, but fell back into being the old Corinne?

"Baby—I mean Sandee—why not your place?" continued Hank. "It's closer than mine."

"No," Corinne answered, to Hank *and* to her fears. "No, no, no." She wasn't taking Hank back to her place. She wasn't returning to the old Corinne.

After an awkward pause, Hank murmured, "Just drop me off at the corner of Doyle and Thurston."

Ten minutes later, they dropped off Hank, who waved at Corinne through her closed window, which she didn't acknowledge. The old Corinne would have been nice, even after risking her neck, but she was more determined than ever to be a new Corinne. And if nothing else, the new Corinne was tired of catering to men. Listening to them, coddling them and saving their lives!

Fifteen minutes later, Leo pulled up to the curb outside Sandee's apartment. "I'll walk you to your door."

"Don't bother." She wrestled with the seat belt, muttering a curse when it didn't want to cooperate.

"Stubborn, sometimes," Leo said under his breath, reaching over and neatly disconnecting the clasp from its socket.

"Only when necessary."

"I was talking about the seat belt."

"So was I." Corinne got out and shut the door. She headed briskly around the car, but didn't beat Leo to the curb. No, he'd jumped out and was keeping up with her, determined no doubt to walk her to the door come hell or high water. "Stubborn, aren't you?"

"Got it from my seat belt."

She huffed a response, determined not to be

amused. At the door, she fumbled in her bag for the keys.

"Door looks good," Leo noted, jiggling the knob to ensure it'd been properly fixed.

The memory of his primal act, breaking open a door to get to her, turned her insides liquid. Darn him, anyway. She was determined to hold on to her anger, to not get aroused. It didn't help that he stood so close. Too close. Honest to God, she felt the heat of his body along the entire length of hers. It saturated her clothes, flamed her skin.

She glanced at him just as he turned to face her. For a lightning moment, they shared a look. She glanced quickly back down into her purse and pulled out the set of jangling keys. Her hands were shaking. With great effort, she managed to extract the front door key and insert it into the lock. As she clicked it open, Leo spoke.

"Didn't know you were a bump and runner."

She paused, then pulled the key out of the lock. Turning, slowly, she met his gaze. "How dare you."

"How dare *me?*"

"You wanted it as bad as I did."

A look of bewilderment crossed his face. "Wanted what?"

Unbelievable. *Insults me, then feigns innocence.* Just like Tony. Her anger kicked up a notch.

"Wanted what?" Leo repeated.

"What you broke the door for." She stepped inside and slammed it shut. Stomping through the living room, she made a mental note to put something over that decorative window, too, after Leo left. The irony of working at Universal Shower Door, and that fricking pane of glass, didn't escape Corinne as she headed into the bedroom.

Leo stood, staring through the glass, watching the blurred image of Sandee walk away. Maybe the image was hazy, but her attitude was clear. *Self-righteous.* Well, maybe he shouldn't have accused her of being a bump-and-run con, but he needed to ask, throw her off guard, see her reaction.

"Well, I certainly got that," he muttered, scratching his beard. What had she said? "You wanted it as bad as I did?" He pondered that riddle for a moment. After mentally testing several answers, all illogical, the only thing that made sense was she didn't know what he meant by "bump and run." Or she was a very, very good liar.

But it didn't add up. Leo headed back down the walk, wishing the jasmine-scented breezes would clear his head of dead-end clues so he could solve this mystery. Was she a liar? He'd dealt with a lot of them, and ninety-nine percent of the time, they were cool under fire because one angry, thoughtless response could crack their mask of deception. On the other hand, someone telling the truth typically got mad, indignant even, because they had nothing to hide. Their emotions were honest because they were.

The way Sandee had been tonight.

He reached the Mustang and got inside. Then it hit him. "VD, that bozo from Denver called her 'Corinne,' which I'd almost chalked up to his being crazy. But when Hank—her former boyfriend, or I guess it's former—calls her 'Baby,' she seems to hate it. You'd think a guy trying to woo back his lady would know what mush terms she likes." *Corinne. Baby.*

Something nagged at him. Something more to do with words. Bingo! He snapped his fingers, recalling Hank's comment. *Since when did you start using such big words?* Sandee, it appeared, didn't talk the way she used to.

Leo snagged the clue. Was Sandee actually someone else...maybe this Corinne from Denver?

If so, he was chasing the wrong suspect.

BR-R-RING. BR-R-RING.

Corinne stared at the phone, which had been ringing every few minutes ever since she'd gotten home. *Darn Sandee anyway, why doesn't she have caller ID?* At least she had a phone machine, so Corinne could get messages, but picking up the phone was like playing Russian Roulette. It could be anybody on the other end. Crazy Hank, crazy Tony or some other crazy man in Sandee's life.

Or it might be Leo, who wasn't exactly crazy except when breaking doors. Or making inappropriate comments like "didn't know you were a bump and runner."

How dare he.

The phone stopped ringing. Corinne glared at it a moment longer, then returned to her spaghetti sauce. She stirred so hard, some of it sloshed onto the stove. Angry, she reached for a paper towel, pulling off at least ten and wrestling with the mess before ripping a hunk loose. Gripping a basketball-sized wad of towels, she blotted at the small splotch of red, furious at the sloshing sauce, furious at the paper towels...

But really, really furious at that smug, brazen Leo whatever-his-last-name-was for being so *rude.*

Throwing the wad into the trash, Corinne muttered, "Accusing *me* of being a bump and runner. And to think a few days ago I couldn't excite my fiancé. But let me finally excite one other man, and I'm a... a...harlot!" It was just so unfair. A woman tries to look like a hot dish with her fiancé, and she ends up feeling—and looking—like plastic-wrapped leftovers. But let her get the hots for a new guy, the *second* man she's ever been with in her *entire* life, and she gets a reputation.

She's called a "bump and runner."

Br-r-ring. Br-r-ring.

Who's so insistent? This time, the sound was a welcome distraction to her mood. *Maybe it's Sandee.* Good! Corinne was ready for the real Sandee to come home...and the real Corinne, whoever that was, to embark on her new life. Setting the spoon onto a piece of paper towel, which had somehow discretely separated during the thrashing melee, Corinne headed to the pink wall phone.

"Hello?"

"*Mi amante,* I'm so sorry..."

Hank. She debated whether to hang up.

"I'm heartbroken over the pain I've caused you. I've been stupid because I'm losing you, the woman I love."

Well, maybe she'd listen for a little bit.

"I'm a no-good lover, a no-good criminal because I'm bungling both..."

No-good criminal?

"...making you bump and run, then trying to pull that again tonight..."

What was it with Vegas-ites? Didn't anybody say the word "sex" in this part of the country? Plus nobody on this planet could *make* Sandee do anything, especially bumping and running. That woman did what she wanted, when she wanted. As Hank continued to ramble on with grief-stricken confessions and love-talk, Corinne wondered why he said "trying to pull that again tonight." He hadn't tried to bump and run her. He'd hinted he wanted to come over, but that was hardly a sexual advance.

She tightened her grip on the phone and listened intently.

"...I'm going to turn myself in to the police, prove to you I can change my ways, be a better man, a man worthy of your love..."

What had he called himself? A "no-good criminal"? And now he's saying he'll turn himself in to the police? Ah-hah. Corinne got it. *Sandee didn't run away because of a broken heart, she ran away because this guy did something bad. Something...criminal?* But Hank was also very emotional, so it was difficult to know how much of this confession was exaggerated...

"I'd climb the highest mountain," Hank pleaded.

Next, he'd be fighting a tycoon. Whatever had happened, this guy had it bad for her cousin. And Corinne knew Sandee loved Hank, too. They needed to discuss this without Corinne in the middle.

When he took a breath, Corinne jumped in. "Hank, are you sitting down?"

Pause. "*Sí*. Yes."

She took in a deep breath. "Because I'm not who you think I am. And after I explain everything to you, I have a phone number I want you to call..."

"I WANT SANDEE!"

Leo stood in the kitchen, his hand on the refrigerator handle. In the last twenty-four hours, he'd experienced passion, betrayal and mind-numbing confusion. A package of emotions almost as intense as the moods he'd experienced in the last year. He needed some serious down time. "Not tonight, Mel. Let's play a new tune."

Squawk. "I want Sandee!"

"I should never have said her name," Leo grumbled. "I'll be on my deathbed, and the last words I'll hear will be—" He caught himself before saying it. No way he'd encourage that bird. Leo shot a look at Mel, perched on the kitchen counter. "What happened to Merlot? I thought you wanted Merlot?"

Mel cocked his green-feathered head. "Merlot," he repeated, hobbling over to the wine rack with that peg-legged pirate walk.

"Good," Leo whispered, pulling on the fridge handle and helping himself to a soda. "He's off that Sandee kick." He squeezed shut his eyes, ready to kick himself for that slip.

Tap tap tap.

Leo turned. Mel was industriously pecking at the cork in one of the wine bottles. Great. This old trick. Leo closed the refrigerator door and crossed to the wine rack where Mel was pecking. "Good luck, buddy. It'll take you longer to work your way through that cork than it would a prisoner to dig his way out with a spoon." Shaking his head, Leo walked into the living room, listening to the incessant tap tap tap behind him.

"Mel," he called out, "you're more obstinate than I am." He started to take a swig of soda.

"I want Sandee!"

Leo halted, holding the can midair. "Or maybe not." He headed into the living room and sank into his leather chair, which creaked with his weight. The flutter of wings. Mel landed on the TV tray that doubled as a coffee table.

Leo blew out a puff of air. "All this is your fault, you know."

Squawk!

"Yes, it is. You and I hanging out day after day, griping and drinking, was like a bad remake of *Grumpy Old Men*. I had to go back to work before I started squawking and flying."

"Hey, good-lookin'!"

"Don't change the subject." Leo stood, began pacing. "Dom said I wasn't ready for the streets, stuck me with desk duty. Four months later, I thought I'd lose my mind if I had to file one more report or answer one more ringing phone. I didn't ask, I damn near begged for a chance to play detective again. Dom gives me an easy gig. Studebaker bump and run." Leo took a long drink, savoring the fizzy lemon taste. "Now here I am, two days on the job, clueless as to the whereabouts of the Studebaker...but I have a stolen Ferrari and a crashed Tracker. That should impress Dom."

"I want Sa—"

"And that's your fault, too! Last night, I was trying to watch the news, spend some quality guy time with you, but no. You have to keep bringing her up, making me think about her, want her...and I end up going over to her place and falling in love—" Ho-o boy, *that* one slipped out.

He sank back into the leather chair. "Maybe I've been alone so long that the first woman I'm with, I fall for."

Mel flew to the arm of the chair, where he perched and looked intently at Leo.

"Now you're going to listen, encourage me to confess more, huh?" Leo rubbed Mel on the head. "I can't love her, Mel. I don't even know who she is..."

But he did. He'd seen her affection for children at the supermarket when she'd danced with that rattle. Seen her passion, and vulnerability, when they'd made love. Seen her spunk tonight when she'd put him and Hank on notice that no man was going to order her around. He knew she was a tender woman, a strong woman.

Just as he knew she wasn't Sandee.

He scrubbed a hand along his beard, realizing they'd both been wearing disguises. In a sense, they'd both been undercover. If he was being more logical, he'd back off. But it was too late. He'd fallen for the woman underneath that Sandee disguise...and he had to know who she was, and why she was playing this game, before he'd give up. He'd lost a lot this past year, and right or wrong, what he felt with this woman was the first real thing to come into his life in a long, long time.

Leo stood. "I have to know who she really is, Mel," he said, setting his soda on the TV tray.

LEO APPROACHED THE apartment door. The textured pane of glass glowed from the blaze of lights in the apartment. Good. Lights on meant she was up. He checked his watch. Midnight. Well, she was accustomed to men showing up at this hour, so he wasn't exactly being rude.

Although, earlier, she'd treated him as though he were the rudest dog on the planet. Her response, "You wanted it as bad as I did," left him clueless as to what *exactly* she'd taken offense at. Not an uncommon predicament for the human male species when dealing with the female species. To get back in her good graces, he needed to clear the air, apologize. Then he'd ask her, tactfully, just who the hell she really was.

Of course, first he had to pass the peephole test. Look apologetic, sincere, remorseful. He'd never looked any of those things in his life, but he'd give it his best shot.

He knocked. And waited.

No answer.

Through the glass pane, he looked for movements. Nothing.

He knocked again.

Still, no answer.

"I shoulda pulled a Brawny Baker and brought her a pan of something," Leo muttered. "Too bad I don't cook." *But I could have picked up some flowers or a gift.* He toyed with the idea of jogging back to the car and getting VD, but nixed it. With Leo's recent history, he'd give away his voodoo buddy and end up with ten years of bad luck. Plus, he'd miss his car pal. He, Mel, and VD had become a sort of family this past year.

He checked his watch again. Twelve-ten. He glanced through the opaque window. No movement.

Keeping all those lights on, "Sandee" must have one whopper of an electric bill. But all those lights at midnight? Didn't make sense.

Also didn't make sense that she hadn't come to the door yet.

Was she okay? Leo's mind went into overdrive. Had Hank shown up, even though she'd told him she didn't want his company? Or, worse, had that bozo Tony shown up and forced his way inside?

Leo tested the door knob. Locked. Okay, he was glad the damn thing had been fixed, but he didn't like being locked out...not knowing if she was okay. He took a deep breath and expelled it. Time to act rationally. Last time he'd been out of control and broken the damn lock—this time he'd force it open, gently. He pulled out his wallet and extracted a credit card. An old trick, but one he'd once perfected...

A few moments later, he opened the door. He quickly stepped inside and shut it behind him. Hardly breaking and entering considering he had justifiable cause to be concerned for her safety. He looked around the front room. Last night he'd been too preoccupied with her to be aware of the surroundings. Now he saw it had the same peachy color as her bedroom. Peachy and pink. Last night he'd had the passing thought that it didn't seem her style. Now he knew why. Because this place had been decorated by somebody else—the real Sandee, most likely.

He scanned the area, looking for signs of a scuffle. None. Everything looked tidy, even the stack of ladies' magazines was neatly arranged. He caught "Sandee's" signature rose scent. And another smell...spaghetti sauce? He headed across the pink carpet, which ended at a square faux-wood floor on which sat a small glass table and chairs. Dining room. Kitchen had to be back here...he passed the table and headed through the swinging door. Bingo. On the stove was a pan filled with sauce, but otherwise, everything looked undisturbed.

Something in the trash caught his eye.

He stepped toward a heap of white sticking out of the plastic pink—of course!—trash can. The mass of white was a pile of paper towels...*streaked with red*. Panic slammed through him. He raced toward the bedroom. Entering the hallway, he heard the rushing sound of water. Shower? He glanced at the bathroom door, which was wide open.

The shower doors were clear, like looking through a window. She was sudsing herself, rubbing her hands over her body. Memories of that body, how it felt, how it moved, shot through his mind. She hummed a tune, which faded in and out with the hush of shower spray. Her voice was sweet, melodic.

Go. Don't stand here, watching. You'll frighten her.

Too late. She turned and froze. Those gray eyes widened.

He hated himself for scaring her. He was rude; he was a cad.

"I'm sorry," he said. He opened his hands, as though that did any good. What was he trying to prove? That he didn't have anything up his sleeves? "I'm sorry," he repeated.

If she didn't hear, she had to see the look on his face. He'd been right to be concerned for her safety, but he'd been wrong to stand here and watch her, uninvited, in the privacy of her shower. Maybe before he didn't know how to look apologetic, but he sure did now. He turned to go.

The shower stopped. "Leo, wait. Please."

That voice. Sweet. Urgent. He turned, slowly. She'd pressed herself against the shower door, the look in her eyes both sad and hot. He looked down at her luscious breasts, their fullness pressed against the glass. Blood roared in his ears. She stepped back and slid open the door, removing the barricade between them. When she stepped out of the shower, it was all he could do to stay put. He slipped his thumbs into his waistband, mainly to stop his hands from taking action before his mind—whatever part hadn't melted down—could logically dictate his next steps.

Her pink skin glistened with shower spray. Her hair clung in wet strands to her cheek, her neck. Drops of water traced sensuous, lazy paths down her body...

To hell with logic. An invisible, powerful current pulled him forward. He gathered her in his arms, savoring her clean, soapy scent, the wet silkiness of her flesh. So good. So warm. "I knocked. No answer. I got worried—"

She silenced him with a soft finger against his mouth. "I've never seen a man so worried..."

A wet curl straggled over her eye. He pulled it back, then held her head with his hands, studying her face. "You're...so...beautiful."

And when she looked pleased, those gray eyes yielding, softening to a smoky color, he wanted more. He burrowed his lips into the bend of her neck and inhaled deeply. *There.* That hint of rose, her signature scent. Like her truest self, sweet and pure. He moved his lips across her cheek, settling onto her lips, which opened like a full blossom.

Corinne drank in his kiss, letting his passion meld with hers. When he pulled back, she liked how desire changed his face. Last night, in the shadows, it had been difficult to see him, read his reactions. But tonight she saw how passion altered his features, easing the harshness. She traced a finger along his lips, enjoying how her touch caused one side of his mouth to kick up in that lopsided grin.

"Whatever I said earlier...I'm sorry," he whispered huskily.

Tony never apologized, even when his infidelity was shoved in her face, he never once said "I'm sorry." But Leo, different story. She couldn't deny her anger had flared earlier on the doorstep...and again when he'd surprised her in the shower, but seeing his tender look, hearing his apology, her resolve melted. "I didn't like what you called me..."

His brow furrowed. "Bump and runner?"

She nodded. "What we shared last night was special, not something to be denigrated."

He started to speak, then stopped. "I'm not making the connection." He held her tighter, as though afraid she might bolt again, although where did he think she'd go, stark naked? "Bump and run has nothing to do with what happened last night."

"It doesn't?"

He laughed, a low throaty chuckle. "Honey, just what do you think 'bump and run' means?"

"Isn't it another term for...sex?"

"No!" He gave her a puzzled look before leaning back, laughing fully, the sound rich, velvety. God, she loved his laughter. He looked back down, his eyes shining. "So *that's* what you thought. No wonder..." He gave his head a shake. "For the record, what happened last night was making love, not sex. And now I know for certain that you're not..." He searched her face, the green of his eyes deepening to the color of the sea.

"I'm not what?"

His fingertips grazed along the sides of her body, their roughened touch teasingly sensuous. "The real question is, what are you doing standing here, gorgeously naked, talking?"

She smiled. "And what should I be doing?"

"Bumping and running?" he answered with a saucy wink, taking her hand and leading her toward the bedroom.

11

"THIS BUMP AND RUNNER is gonna run to the kitchen and get us some snacks." Corinne bounded out of bed and scampered from the room. Leo *still* hadn't explained the real meaning of "bump and run"—heck, there hadn't been time for conversation ever since his surprise visit during her shower! She'd never seen a guy feel so sorry, so bad. Down-and-out, put-me-in-the-doghouse bad.

Only a woman with a stone cold heart would have let him go.

And it's a good thing she hadn't, because now she knew at least what "bump and run" *didn't* mean. It didn't mean *sex*. So earlier, on the porch, he hadn't been putting her down. In fact, now she liked playing with the term.

And speaking of playing...her insides did funny twisty things just recalling every steamy-hot, gimme-more-more-*more* thing they'd done tonight...

No wonder she was ravenous. They'd probably burned up hundreds, no *thousands*, of calories. Giggling, she half-slid, half-traipsed across the smooth kitchen floor to open the refrigerator. *I never felt hungry after being with Tony. But then, he never made me feel as though he couldn't get enough of me. In five years with Tony, I never felt as beautiful and sexy as I have with Leo in the last...*she quickly calculated...*twenty-seven hours.*

Funny. Before, she never remembered exact numbers, either. It was always five years, give or take a few months. Ten pounds, give or take. But when it came to Leo, she could be a hot number and calculate them too, like a Certified Public Accountant. She glanced at the clock on the stove. Yep, they'd been lovers twenty-seven hours and ten minutes. That man made her want to remember every delicious minute of their togetherness.

Humming one of her favorite Céline Dion tunes, Corinne threw together a snack tray, thanking the Supermarket Powers That Be she'd found that store the other night. She laid out some of that fancy-shmantzy goat cheese, a handful of crackers, several orange and apple slices, and the pièce de résistance—marinated artichoke hearts! She stood back and admired the assortment. "*Much* better than a bunch of leftovers," she murmured. She'd have to give Sandee some snack-tray tips when her cousin returned in a few days.

A few days. For a moment, Corinne's confidence wavered. In a few days, who would she be? She could never return to her old life...but who was the new Corinne? Whoever it was, she knew in her heart, that that was the woman Leo had been making love to.

She picked up the tray. "And as for myself, I have forty-eight hours to figure out my new life's direction," she whispered, carrying the tray back to the bedroom...

...She nearly dropped the tray at the sight of Leo sitting up in bed, his gorgeous torso rising above the bunched covers like one of those mythological gods rising, bare-chested, out of the sea. All muscle and bulk carpeted with wild swirls of chest hair. She gripped the tray tighter, remembering how deliciously wanton she'd felt burying her face in that hair, inhaling his masculine scent, licking and kissing sunburnt skin...

"What are you looking at?" he asked.

"Your chest," she answered, in a strange voice that had more squeak than substance. She cleared her throat. "It's a nice chest." Nice? "Great, actually. Like one of those sea gods rising out of the ocean." She squeezed shut her eyes, wishing she'd had the sense to stop at "Great." *I might as well wear a sign saying, Woman Who Spent Years Not Being Properly Laid.*

She opened her eyes. Her reaction seemed to amuse him. "Thank you. I think." He looked around. "Although I've never seen a peach-colored ocean before."

"Peach?" She looked at the satin-trimmed bedspread and gave her head a shake. "Definitely tangerine." She crossed to the bed and set the tray in the middle. "Tangerine becomes you."

Leo reached over and cupped one breast. "And being naked becomes you."

The appreciative gleam in his eyes caused a self-conscious heat to fill her cheeks.

"You're blushing."

"You make me feel so...so nice." *Nice? Here I go again, wearing that invisible sign, fumbling with words as though I just learned to speak.* If she'd had her wits about her, she'd have said "You make me feel so scrumptious, beautiful, meltdown-hot desirable!" because *that's* how Leo really made her feel. But rather than attempt the English language again, she scooted to her side of the bed and got in.

"Tangerine," he murmured, checking out the tray of food. "Is that your favorite color?"

"It's hers—I mean mine."

He looked up. "Hers?"

Corinne made a mental note not to speak for several hours after having meltdown sex. "Hers. Right. I meant my friend who helped me decorate." She quickly picked up a slice of orange and crammed it in her mouth before she said something else incriminating.

"So you call this color tangerine?" He looked around. "I'd say it's peach."

Corinne wiped some juice off her chin. "You say peach, I say tangerine?"

"Tomato, toe-maah-toe..." He did that lopsided grin again that made her stomach do crazy flip-flops. "Let's call the whole thing off?"

It was lighthearted, this playful talk, but her heart lurched. If Leo knew she was masquerading as someone else, he probably *would* call it off. Problem was, it had never been Corinne's style to lie. Pretending to be her cousin these last few days had at first been exciting...and now, downright exhausting—she'd crack, blurt the truth, sooner or later.

Better sooner. In her gut, she sensed that if she didn't come clean with Leo, she chanced losing the best thing that had ever walked into her life. She knew without a doubt he'd made love to the real her, so it was only fair to divulge her real name, and the real situation. She fidgeted with the bed cover. "I, uh, have something to tell you."

Leo popped an artichoke in his mouth. Chewing, he nodded for her to continue.

"I'm not Sandee." Corinne drew in a deep breath, waiting for some dangerous, intense response.

Instead, he reached for another artichoke. "These are great!"

Okay, she'd expected intense, but not over an artichoke. *Probably didn't hear what I said.* "Leo. I'm not Sandee," Corinne repeated more slowly.

"Um-mmm," he mumbled, enjoying the artichoke. After swallowing, he said, "What kind of cheese is this?"

She paused. "Goat."

He cringed. "I'll pass." As he reached for a cracker, she grabbed his hand.

"Are you ignoring me?"

He raised her hand and kissed it. "Honey, I couldn't ignore you if my life depended on it. You said you weren't Sandee." He shrugged. "I already knew that. And I fibbed when I said I knew Tony, so you and I are even in the not-quite-the-truth category."

How could he be so cool, so blasé about all this! She had half a mind to force-feed him some of that goat cheese. "Well, I knew you didn't know Tony, so...so there." Okay, she wasn't so cool and blasé, but she wasn't about to let him have the last word. She picked up the cracker he'd been reaching for, smeared goat cheese all over it, and popped it into her mouth.

"So you didn't fall for my 'Tony sent me' line?"

She shook her head no. Then yes. After swallowing, she answered, "Well, at first, maybe."

"And why not after that?"

"Because if you really knew Tony, you'd know why he called me Corinne."

"Why?"

"Because that's my name." She breathed in and out, letting the immense relief wash over her. Relief to be herself again. "Corinne McCourt," she added, saying her full name. Although, in a funny way, it was as though she were saying it for the first time. She opened her eyes, feeling another ah-hah moment, but this one more thoughtful than the others. Of course it felt like the first time. She was definitely on her way to being a new person, a new Corinne.

Leo reached over and took her hand. "How do you do, Corinne McCourt."

"And how do you do, Leo—?"

"Wolfman. Leo Wolfman."

Corinne smiled. "I've never been naked with a man, for the second time—well, technically, the third—before finally getting around to formal introductions."

"Me, too. Well, except for the man part." He winked.

"So now that we know I'm Corinne and you're Leo, what's a bump and runner?"

Leo paused. "Someone who steals cars."

"Steals cars?" A light bulb went on. "You think I stole that Ferrari!"

He looked intently at her, then nodded.

"Well, you're right!" She started laughing. "But he stole it back!" And the next thing she knew, she was telling the whole story of *How to Make Your Man Howl*, discovering Tony's infidelity and burning rubber as she drove off in Baby. "…then Sandee suggested I fill in for her at work and overnight I went from Inconspicuous Corinne, payroll girl, to Exotic Sandee, ring-card babe!" She paused to take a breath.

"Here," Leo said, spreading more goat cheese on

another cracker. "You need this to keep up your strength." He fed her. "If you're half as good at payroll as you are in the ring, you're one helluva payroll girl." Leo swept a strand of hair off her forehead. "You returning to that job?"

"No." Actually, she hadn't known for certain until this very instant. But there was no reason to return to Denver. That home had been Tony's—his furniture, his taste, his stuff. Just as the only family was his family because her mom now lived in Florida. Her best pal Kyle lived in Denver, but his partner hated her, so that wasn't a whole lot of incentive to return. Which left her with her job. And the last thing she wanted to do was grow old at Universal Shower Door. To spend her life evolving from payroll girl to payroll little old lady. The thought filled her with cold dread.

"So what's next in the life of Corinne McCourt?"

"A car. A job. A real life." Her voice cracked on the last one because she didn't have the vaguest what that might be.

"Hey," Leo said, pulling her close. "It's okay."

At first she stiffened, not wanting to give in to her insecurities. After all, she hadn't been through all this just to fall apart at the first bit of sympathy to come her way. But when he wrapped his arms around her, murmuring words of comfort, she sank against him, grateful for his strength. And more than willing to fall apart because, damn it, she'd earned it.

After a few moments, Leo said gently, "You were very brave to jump into that Ferrari and drive, spur of the moment, to a new life."

She sucked in a shuddery breath. "Yeah. A terrifying ride considering I had no clothes, no money, no clue as to what I was doing."

Rubbing his face against hers, he whispered into her ear, "Wrong. You cut loose, sped to your destiny. It was a joyride."

Her insides tingled with hope. The first hope she'd felt in days.

He drew back and looked into her eyes. "That's a very impressive story you told. And I've heard a lot of 'em."

"Heard a lot—?" She giggled nervously. "Don't tell me I just spilled my guts to a therapist."

"Close. Detective."

Corinne did a double take. "You're a detective?" She frowned. "So you really did think I'd stolen that Ferrari."

He hesitated. "Sort of."

Corinne gasped as another light bulb or two went on, highlighting things Hank had said. Now it all made sense. "Bump and run. Sandee's boyfriend used that term, too."

"Hank?"

She nodded.

"The guy who brought you that rose, right?"

"He was bringing *Sandee* the rose, not me. That was to make up for asking me to bump and run again—" She stopped. "So that's why you're following Sandee..."

Leo saw the look of painful understanding on Corinne's face. "Yeah, I figured you knew why Sandee had split town." He paused, weighing his words carefully. "I didn't want to bring it up now, after making love. Tonight let's be us, no games, no façades. It's been so long, Corinne, since I've...I don't want to dilute this with the world's worries. Trust me, they'll be waiting for us when we leave here."

Corinne pressed her lips together, a look of anxiety in her gray eyes.

"I mean that," Leo said, stroking her face. "And to prove it, I'm changing the subject. I don't know what's next in the life of Leo Wolfman, either."

The look in her eyes softened.

"You ran your finger along my chest scar last night...that's where I got shot a year ago. That's when my old life ended and a new one began."

"So you know how that feels," she whispered.

Leo laughed, although it wasn't a sound of joy. "Oh, honey, I know how that feels and a whole lot more. I was pretty messed up. Diagnosed with post-traumatic stress syndrome. Spent months unable to sleep, to control my rage, to work. Always had a gnawing feeling in my gut..." Which he suddenly realized he didn't have anymore. The feeling he'd once held on to, like some kind of bizarre life preserver, had disappeared. He didn't need Dr. Denise to know that bad feeling was replaced by something good, something wonderful...something called Corinne.

"What'd you do?"

"Hmm?" He refocused back on Corinne's velvety gray eyes.

"During that tough time—what'd you do?"

"Drank a lot with my parrot."

Corinne paused, then giggled. "No, really."

"Yes, really. I'm okay now, but if Mel—my parrot—doesn't get his act together, I'll have to take him to AA." He liked hearing her laugh again. It was like a girl's. Light, carefree. He was glad he'd finally met the real Corinne McCourt. "I went back to work a few months ago." He shifted, not wanting to stay on that topic. "But, to be honest, I've lost my heart for detective work. What I really want to do is jump into my Silver Bullet...my trailer...and discover the new frontier. One with a small ranch. That's my dream."

"Nothing to keep you here?"

"Nothing," he said flatly. "No furniture, no wife, no family. Lost them all along the way."

"Wife?"

Didn't want to talk about that, either, but he wanted to wipe away that look of discomfort in Corinne's eyes. "Her name was Elizabeth," he said matter of factly. "Last I heard, she moved to L.A., which is where my furniture is unless she sold it."

"Divorced?"

"Yes, and I plan to stay that way." He heard the edge in his voice, but couldn't control it. "After what I've been through, I never want to tie my life to somebody else. She took everything, including my dreams of kids, matching rockers on the porch when we're old. Maybe I'll love again, but I'm not signing any papers."

Corinne felt a little awkward, having this conversation after making love, but she knew how it felt to be betrayed, too. "Well, my dream wasn't concrete like a Silver Bullet and a ranch..." She hesitated. "I wanted a baby..."

Leo squeezed her hand. "I wanted two. Or three."

Corinne giggled softly. "I'd even take four." But despite her lighthearted comment, the old pain resurfaced. How desperately she'd wanted to get pregnant...how disappointing that her husband-to-be hadn't cared. "Let's not talk about dreams anymore," she whispered. "Or Tony or Elizabeth or all the other things that hurt in life."

Leo pulled her close. "Deal."

As they held each other in silence, Corinne determined that if nothing else came out of this, she'd hold on to the gift Leo had given her. That driving from Denver to Vegas hadn't been a desperate escape. It'd been a joyride.

And when he nuzzled closer and buried a kiss at the base of her throat, she willingly succumbed to every dormant desire the old Corinne had buried...and the new Corinne eagerly embraced. "Take me," she whispered hungrily.

KNOCK KNOCK KNOCK.

Corinne listened. Was Leo here already? She glanced at Sandee's bathroom clock, an oval chrome object with rhinestones instead of numbers. Five-thirty. "This morning, Leo said he'd be back tonight at seven," she murmured, grabbing her cousin's silky black robe and throwing it on. Heading to the front door, she tied the sash around her middle, smiling to herself. *Maybe he wanted to catch me early and reenact our shower scene.*

She looked through the peephole at a pair of brown eyes. "Hank," she said through the door, trying not to sound disappointed. "Sandee gets back tomorrow."

"I know. I wanted to see you, Corinne."

He knew her name. Of course, he and Sandee must have discussed Corinne during their phone call last night—the call Corinne asked Hank to make after she confessed she wasn't Sandee. "I'm getting ready to go out," Corinne said, hoping he'd take the hint she didn't have time to talk. She wanted to get dolled up for her first real date with Leo.

"It'll only take two minutes, then I'll go."

From what she'd witnessed, it took him two minutes just to say his name. But he sounded so sad, so earnest. Corinne tightened the sash and opened the door a crack. "Okay, two minutes." She made a mental note to cut him off at five. "What's up?"

He wore white shorts and a light blue T-shirt that showed off more skin than covered it. He did a half wave, an awkward greeting, then folded his hands in front of him. "Corinne," he began, sounding as though he was starting a speech, "I want to apologize for my behavior. I did bad things, but no more. I promised Sandee I'd be a better man. No more... questionable stuff." He raised one hand as though taking an oath. "And I swear this on my mother's grave, God rest her soul." He crossed himself.

Corinne took advantage of the moment of quiet. "It's all right, Hank, I know you didn't mean to hurt anybody—"

"And I never did! Physically, anyway. But I hurt my baby's heart, and I'm gonna make it up to her, show her I'm a man worthy of her love..."

Uh-oh. Hank was going to start climbing the highest mountain any moment. This could grow into five, ten minutes if she didn't find a way to jump in. When he paused, Corinne said quickly, "I appreciate this, I *really* do, but I have to take a shower and get ready for...something..."

"Right." Hank nodded as though in complete agreement. "That's another thing I promised Sandee. I'm gonna stop talking so much. But before I go, I have one more thing to say."

Corinne eased in a breath. This guy was really trying. "Okay, one more thing."

His eyes grew so moist, she thought he was going to start crying. "I'm gonna make it up to that guy with the Studebaker. The bump and run I hoodwinked Sandee into doin'." Hank gestured broadly, as though his hands were unable to remain contained any longer. "I hit that car and slugged the guy, then put him into Sandee's car and made her drive away. Scared her, scared the old guy. Well, after he came to." Hank sniffed, then gained control of himself. "So not only am I makin' amends to Sandee and you, but also to Willy, the old guy. I'm tuning his Studebaker, installing a new radio and fixing the steering wheel." Hank hung his head sheepishly. "Sorry. Talkin' too much again. But I promised Sandee I'd tell the truth from now on, so I wanted to set the record straight. Probably sounds dumb—a story of a guy and a car and how his life changed."

Hank's story hit home. "Not dumb at all," she said purposefully. "It's like the story of a girl and a car and how her life changed..." And for the second time in the past few days, she summed up what had happened to her. Okay, so she'd wanted to make this conversation short, but these few minutes were important. Leo had taught her that certain life journeys—as difficult, dumb or downright painful they might be—can be viewed as joyrides and she wanted to share that with Hank.

"So, even though you think you were on a desperate ride," she finished, feeling darn near Zen-like, "you learned about yourself, about treating people with respect. View your experience as a joyride." She smiled, waiting for Hank's ah-hah response.

"That sonofa—"

Hardly the ah-hah she'd been expecting.

Hank slammed one fist into another. "What a jerk that Tony dude is. Lovin' a car more than you. What's he gonna do for the rest of his life—have babies, make love and grow old with that hunk of metal?" Red-faced, Hank muttered something in Spanish.

"It's over, it's okay," Corinne quickly said. "You need to focus on Sandee, not me. She loves you very much."

Hank's brown eyes moistened again.

Afraid he might drop to his knees any moment, Corinne plastered on a smile and in her best gotta-go voice said, "Thanks for dropping by. We'll see each other again after Sandee's back..."

Hank beamed at the mention of his love's name. "*Sí.* Yes." He started to leave, then stopped. Looking at Corinne's hair, he murmured, "You and Sandee could be twins...except for your..."

"It's not my real color. It's hot gold, the color of Tony's Ferrari." Corinne shrugged. "Good thing he didn't buy a purple car." She winked and closed the door.

KNOCK KNOCK.

Corinne had just stepped out of the shower. She glanced at the rhinestone-numbered clock. Five minutes after six. Maybe she'd misunderstood the time? Had Leo said six instead of seven?

She glanced in the mirror and fingered her wet, unkempt hair. He liked it last night, so she'd keep it this way. And she'd stay naked, too. No, wait. She'd slip into a pair of Sandee's killer heels and give Leo a little hot-cha-cha surprise.

Knock. Knock.

"Be right there," she called out, slipping into the heels. She nearly ran to the front door, something she certainly couldn't have done a week ago in these things. With a shake of her head, she opened the door and whispered seductively, "Take me."

"You bet," said Tony, looking surprised and lascivious.

Corinne slammed shut the door and leaned against it, catching her breath.

"Baby, open up!"

Baby. He had a lot of nerve. "No! Go away!"

"You look hot, Corinne. Open up, I want to take you."

She felt sick to her stomach. "Tony, it's over. Go home." She felt so damn mad, *she* was ready to kick the door, but that would only encourage Tony to start *his* kicking routine on the other side.

Pause. "Who'd you think was out here?"

She smiled. *Oh-h-h, good.* Mr. Macho was getting a taste of his own medicine. Conspicuous Hot Babe Corinne had opened the door dressed in nothing but a pair of stilettos, expecting another man. The deliciousness of the moment was beyond karma...it was cata-karma-strophic. If revenge was sweet, this was a pure-cane-sugar moment.

"Gone a week," Tony yelled, "and you're already seeing another man?"

"If you kick the door, Tony, I'll call the police."

"Don't need to. I'm here."

Another male voice? Corinne peeked through the hole. The Phantom had appeared, as though by magic. Oh-h-h, this was extra good. Maybe Tony wasn't so smart when it came to women, but he was smart enough to not play macho with The Phantom again.

"Okay, I'm leaving," said Tony tersely. "I only came by to pick up my fiancée and go home."

"I'm not your fiancée anymore, Tony. If you want a fiancée, buy a ring for that frizzy blonde." Corinne grinned, loving this conversation.

"But I love you."

She rolled her eyes. "You have a funny way of showing it."

"I made a mistake."

"A big one." Or two or three…or more. On that long drive to Vegas, Corinne had plenty of time to realize there'd undoubtedly been other women.

"I want to marry you, have a baby."

The words she wanted so desperately to hear almost a week ago. And now, she thanked her lucky stars she hadn't. Because if Tony had said it then, she never would have experienced this joyride to a new life, a new Corinne. "Tony," she said, raising her voice, "you had your chance and you blew it. Now go."

There was a heavy silence.

"You heard the lady," said The Phantom, his voice like rolling thunder. "Go."

Footsteps. Corinne peeked out the hole and saw the

big, hulky guy, his massive arms folded across his chest, which he'd managed to squeeze into a T-shirt decorated with a skull that had flames shooting out of it. No wonder Tony obeyed The Phantom! Which reminded her of something she wanted to ask...

"Phantom?"

He turned and looked at the door. "Yeah?"

"What's your real name?"

He looked perplexed. "Nigel. You know that."

Nigel? Who would have thought a "Nigel" would grow up to be The Phantom? She smiled to herself. "Have I told you lately what a wonderful friend you are?"

Honest to God, he blushed. "No, Sandee."

Corinne would have to coach Sandee on saying some more nice things to Nigel. Not to lead him on, but enough to feed his ego a little. Speaking of feeding, Corinne had almost forgotten. "And thank you for those brownies. They were delicious."

He shuffled his feet and smiled like a kid. "Thanks, Sandee."

"Thank *you*, Nigel."

As Corinne walked back to the bedroom to get dressed, she marveled at how, recently, the pivotal moments of her life seemed to occur on doorsteps. "When one door closes, another opens," she mused, doing a little two step in her killer heels.

Knock knock knock.

Seven-fifteen. Corinne had been darn near pacing waiting for Leo! She crossed to the door and checked the peephole. Although this time she was dressed in a cute little dress she'd found in Sandee's closet, she didn't want to take a chance and open the door to the wrong man.

When she spied those familiar green eyes, her insides did a heated fluttery number. Yes, *this* was the right man. She opened the door and said, "Third time's the charm!"

She'd never seen him this dressed up. Neatly pressed slacks, a short-sleeved green shirt that matched his eyes, and dress shoes. Yummy yummy yummy. No man had the right to look so sexy doing nothing but standing.

Leo stepped inside and gathered her into his arms. "Every time's a charm with you," he responded, burrowing his face into her hair, her neck. "I told you tonight was your night, wherever you wanted to go. Did you pick a place?" he whispered into her ear.

"Yes."

"And?"

"I want to see the Silver Bullet."

AN HOUR LATER, Leo inserted the key into the front door lock of his house. "I apologize ahead of time for my décor. It's not as nice as inside the Bullet, I'm afraid." He'd been surprised at her suggestion to see his trailer, had thought she was joking at first. But no, she'd been adamant that that's what she wanted to do. So he'd spent the last twenty minutes showing her his pride and joy, and all the remodeling he'd done inside, including the new custom-made curtains he'd just installed. She'd been quiet, but her eyes had glistened, which told him she liked what she saw.

He was fairly certain her eyes wouldn't glisten so

much in his TV-tray decorated rental home, however. He opened the door and ushered her in.

She stepped inside and looked around. "It's so..."

"Sparse?" He shut the door, wishing he'd thought to do something hospitable, like maybe buy some root beer so he didn't have only that lemon-flavored soda to offer. But he thought they'd go out to dinner, see a movie...anything but do a tour of the Silver Bullet and his bachelor pad.

"Yes, I guess 'sparse' describes it," Corinne said a little brightly. Too brightly. "Nothing wrong with sparse."

"As I said, Elizabeth got everything." He heard the edge in his voice, but it was too late. Hell, he didn't know how to date. Men who knew how to woo women properly didn't give tours of renovated trailers. "Care for a soda?" Hoped to God she liked lemon.

"Sure," she said, a bit too casually, staring at a TV tray.

"That's my coffee table."

Her gaze shifted to the TV tray on the other side of the leather chair.

"And that's my reading table." Before she looked at the TV tray that doubled for a bookcase, he headed toward the kitchen. "I'll get those sodas."

As he stepped into the kitchen, he noticed Mel in the sink, propped at an angle.

"What're you doing there, buddy?"

Squk!

Hardly Mel's usual hearty squawk. Leo observed how Mel seemed to be staring oddly at the chipped ceramic basin, as though trying to figure out what it was. "You okay, Mel?" Leo smelled something. Tannic.

Wine? He looked around and saw a pile of little brown pieces underneath the wine rack.

Cork?

"What happened?" Leo moved toward the pile of cork, knowing full well what happened. Sure enough, one of the bottles of wine had its cork missing. And, as the bottles were tilted down, there was a pool of wine on the counter.

"Need some help?" Corinne stood in the doorway.

TV trays for furniture. Drunken parrots. Leo Wolfman sure knew how to impress a woman.

"Is that your parrot?" She stepped forward and gasped. "Is he sick?"

"He's, uh, a little tipsy I'm afraid." Leo gently picked up Mel and carried him to his water cup. "Time to sober up, buddy."

"M'lo," Mel said, teetering on his legs next to the cup.

"What'd he say?"

Leo sucked in a breath. "Merlot."

Corinne looked surprised, then serious. "You weren't kidding when you said you and your parrot drank together."

"That was months ago." God, he was acting defensive again. Getting that edge in his voice. "Sorry, I just hadn't expected to come home and discover Mel had learned the fine art of opening wine bottles." He began cleaning up the cork mess. "Sandee, I mean Cor—"

"I want Sandee," Mel croaked.

Corinne gasped. "Did you hear what he said?"

"Uh, yeah." *Should have bought a parakeet.*

She touched his head, stroking it lightly. "Corinne? Can you say Corinne?"

Squk. "I want Sandee."

Leo finished mopping up the wine and cork, then retrieved two sodas from the fridge. "Come on," he said, walking past Corinne and Mel. "Let's go into the living room. Mel's fine. He'll keep drinking water, which is good for him."

In the living room, Leo motioned for Corinne to sit in the leather chair. When he handed her the soda, she asked, "Where will you sit?"

Good question. Considering he'd never had a guest before, it hadn't been an issue. "I'll stand. No problem." He took a quick swig, more for something to do than because he was thirsty.

"I'm sorry," she suddenly said.

"For what?"

"Asking you to bring me here. You're acting so uncomfortable."

"I just wasn't...prepared...but please don't apologize, Sandee."

"I want Sandee!" Mel barked from the other room.

Leo winced. He'd never known himself to make so many slips. Or known Mel to be such a rowdy, keen-eared drunk. Rolling the cold soda between his hands, he said, "Let me toss the rest of the wine bottles, then let's go somewhere, okay?"

Corinne nodded, but Leo caught a wary look on her face as he headed back to the kitchen. He'd seen different sides of her personality, but this was the first time she looked...withdrawn.

At the kitchen door, he turned. "This Sandee stuff...please understand that on several occasions, I said your—I mean her—name, and Mel picked up on it."

She smiled, barely. "It's not Mel, it's you. You're the one who keeps calling me Sandee. For the record, I'm Corinne."

"I know that!" Damn, defensive again.

Corinne faltered. And for the past few days, she'd felt so certain he'd wanted *her*. That he'd made love to *her*. But if he couldn't even get her and her cousin's names straight...maybe he didn't really know Corinne McCourt after all. Maybe the truth was he'd fallen for a ring-card girl named Sandee.

Corinne's joyride had come to a screeching halt, and she'd only just realized it. "I'm Corinne," she whispered.

12

"I'M PREGNANT."

Sandee, sitting on the couch while studiously applying bright pink polish to her toes, froze. "What?"

Corinne fingered the gold heart pendant around her neck. After Sandee returned home, almost two weeks ago, Corinne had started wearing it again. The pendant brought her a certain comfort. "I'm pregnant."

"That's what I thought you said." Sandee set the polish on the coffee table and leveled Corinne a no-nonsense look. "Never a dull moment, huh, cuz? You officially quit your job in Denver, I got a new one at the jewelry boutique. You dumped Tony for good, I'm almost hitched to Hank." Sandee glanced at the small diamond on her ring finger. She looked back at Corinne. "I thought our lives might be settling down, but maybe not!" She patted the couch seat next to her. "Sit yourself down and let's talk."

Which they'd done a lot over the last few weeks. They'd discussed Corinne's short-lived career as a ring-card girl, Tony's short-lived attempt to win Corinne back and Hank's long-term goals to be a better man. Corinne had occasionally mentioned the detective who'd tailed her, but kept the references brief, not divulging the nature of their relationship beyond the surface stuff. Because it hurt to discuss him. What had happened between her and Leo had been hot and fast.

And in the flash of that intense connection, Leo had fallen hard for her sizzling rendition of Sandee.

Corinne sat down, liking how the new yellow shift dress she'd bought billowed slightly as she moved. She'd purchased several new shifts recently—it was either that or wear Sandee's supertight clothes or Geoff's Liza Minelli garb.

Sandee arched one perfectly tweezed eyebrow. "You sure you're pregnant?"

"Unless those little home kits lie, yes."

"You missed your—?"

"I'm exactly one week, five days late. And I'm *never* late." She smiled wryly. "That was the old me, never late, always following rules..."

"But not anymore it appears!" Sandee pursed her pink-glossed lips and blew out a breath. "Wow, Corinne, when you turn your life upside down, you do one hel—I mean, heck of a job." Sandee turned serious. "Do you...want this baby?"

"Are you kidding? It's the one thing I *know* I want in my new life. Everything else is a big question mark but this baby is definite." She leaned back and rubbed her tummy, the tummy that would grow round and full with child. "Maybe this is a surprise, at a time in my life when everything is uncertain, but I can handle it." Whoa. Those words slipped out, yet she knew it was true. "The new Corinne," she said, sitting straighter, "is strong, confident, positive."

"And a little crazy," murmured Sandee. She reached for a cigarette carton lying next to the nail polish, then stopped. "I'll sneak puffs outside, but not in the apartment. Secondary smoke isn't good for mothers-to-be." She tapped one manicured fingernail against the glass coffee table. "I gotta ask. Didn't you practice birth control?"

"Yes." Corinne scrunched up her face, feeling like a kid about to get chastised. "Except for one time..." It had been after their talk on that tangerine-peach morning. Now, looking back, Corinne wondered if her subconscious had orchestrated the whole thing...the subconscious that had never stopped wanting to have a child.

"Who's the father?" Sandee asked, concern shadowing her features. "The guy whose calls you don't return?"

Leo. Corinne felt a pang of remorse. But that night at his place, when he couldn't get her name right, had cleared the smoke from her burning fantasies. That's when she realized he was enamored with her façade, not with the real Corinne McCourt.

And after all she'd been through, the last thing she needed was to fall for a guy who'd find her to be a disappointment when the smoke finally cleared from his eyes. When that happened, she'd shrink back into herself and return to being Inconspicuous Corinne, the timid woman who placed value in those *How to Make Your Man Howl* books instead of herself. She'd already lived that life with Tony. No way would she live like that with another man.

"Earth to Corinne." Sandee lightly touched her cousin's arm.

Corinne blinked. "Sorry, got lost in my thoughts."

"Hon, who's the father?" Sandee repeated.

"You're right." She swallowed back emotion. "It's the guy whose calls I don't return."

"Does he have a name?"

Corinne paused. "Leo," she said softly.

"Is he not fit to be a father?"

"He's recovering from post-traumatic stress something, has a drunk parrot for a pet and an assortment of TV trays for furniture." She smiled sadly. "But the real reason I don't think he's right for me is that he thinks I'm...you."

Sandee blinked her false eyelashes. "Wait a minute...you didn't...and let him think..."

"No! Well, not really. I mean, we made love and I thought he didn't know I was me, but he did, or said he did, which surprised me until he explained that he knew I wasn't you." Corinne waved her hands in the air. "Forget that part. I think he fell for the me who wore those illegal bikinis and pranced around in skyscraper heels...in other words, he fell for you."

"I don't prance."

"You know what I mean. He fell for exciting, uninhibited, sexy Sandee."

"But..." Sandee tapped her finger against her bottom lip "...all those things are you, too, cuz. It's always been there, hidden maybe. You just let it float to the top for a while."

Corinne hadn't really thought of that before. That her sexy behavior wasn't something contrived, but a part of her she'd finally revealed. "He had trouble remembering my name, though. Kept slipping up, calling me Sandee."

Her cousin looked thoughtful for a moment. "Well, Tony still calls every other day. You could always go back to him."

"When hell freezes over."

"Well, I see the *new* Corinne doesn't shy away from

expressing herself colorfully." With a conspiratorial giggle, Sandee squeezed her cousin's hand. "Anyway, Tony's more unstable than ever after that old guy did a bump and run on him driving back to Denver—"

"Remember how furious he was when he called to tell me, wanting sympathy, and all I could do was laugh?" Corinne giggled. "Isn't karma something? He lost Baby." She patted her stomach. "But look who's got her own." She snapped her fingers. "Ah-hah!"

"Ah-hah?"

"I have my baby. I have me. I'm going to *be* what I've always wanted to be. A mom. Why do I need a man, too?"

"But...you don't have a job...or a place to live..."

"If I want a security blanket, I'll buy one. I don't need a man to fill that role." Corinne stretched back against a couch pillow. "You know, I just read this great interview with Angelina Jolie, who always reminded me of you by the way. She said her greatest insight was when she realized she was free. And right now, I'm realizing I'm *free.* No more impossible rules to live by for me. After what I've been through, I can do anything. I can *always* get a payroll job. I'll probably have to take a loan from mom to get my own place, but I'll pay her back. I'll make ends meet for me and my baby." She breathed in and out, deeply. "Me and my baby...I love how that sounds."

Br-ring. Br-ring.

"And I love how that sounds," Sandee said drolly, heading to the phone. "Betcha five bucks it's Leo again, asking for you. Maybe he slipped and called you Sandee, but he's been asking for Corinne ever since."

KNOCK KNOCK.

Corinne looked at the wall clock. 2:00 p.m. After her confession earlier this morning, Sandee announced they'd spend the rest of the day taking it easy. A "chill" day for Sandee, Corinne, and baby. So they'd spent hours listening to music, reading magazines, napping.

And now somebody was knocking on the door. "Were you expecting someone?" Corinne asked her cousin, who shook her head no.

"Maybe Nigel baked more brownies," mused Sandee. "Since you told me to be nicer to him, he's been baking more than ever!" She set down her magazine, crossed to the door and peeked through the security hole. "No, looks like a deliveryman."

She answered, and after exchanging a few pleasantries, signed something, and shut the door. Carrying a large envelope back into the living room, she said, "Listen to what's written on this. 'For the woman whose body is better than any ol' Ferrari's.'" Sandee looked up. "Ferrari. Tony. Is he trying a new technique to woo you back?"

Corinne groaned. "Hope not. Anyway, doesn't sound like Tony."

"Sounds like it's for you, though." Sandee crossed the room and handed her cousin the envelope.

Corinne opened it and stared inside. She felt her mouth drop open. After a moment, she opened the envelope wide for her cousin to see.

Sandee gasped. "Look at all that moola!" She dipped her manicured nails inside, pulled out a wad of bills and began counting. After a few moments, she whispered, "I'm holding at *least* five grand."

Corinne stared at the wads of hundred-dollar bills. "There's got to be ten times that in the envelope."

"It's like some fairy godmother knew you were going to need money for the baby!" Sandee crowed, tossing a handful into the air. But then she turned thoughtful, tapped her finger on her bottom lip. "Uh-oh. It's cash."

Corinne sighed. "Doesn't take a rocket scientist to see this money is from whoever sold Tony's Ferrari on the black market, does it?" She shoved bills back into the envelope. "I can't keep this."

"Oh yes you can," Sandee began, but a wary look came into her eye. "I think this 'old guy' had some behind-the-scenes help stealing the Ferrari. There's no one to give the money back to but you, cuz...but I'm calling Hank." She sashayed toward the phone. "He better not be behind this 'cause he *swore* to me he was going straight!"

"THERE SHE GOES, VD," Leo said quietly, watching Corinne pull out of the garage in a pink convertible. Pink. He winced. Had to belong to Sandee, the one who'd decorated her apartment in shades of tangerine, peach and pink. "Somebody should force that woman to check out the rest of the color wheel," he muttered.

Leo had avoided coming around here because he hadn't felt welcome. Hard to get the warm fuzzies when you're always told someone isn't "available." But he knew better than to show up and demand she talk to him. If Corinne wouldn't do that on the phone, she wouldn't do that in person, either.

So he'd decided to wait until Corinne left, then ask Sandee why her cousin was freezing him out.

Walking up to the door brought back a flood of memories. Some of them amusing, like the Brawny Baker with that pan or Hank on his knees, pleading passionately. But the best memories were of Corinne. Tender, sweet memories. In his mind, he saw her in that long pink T-shirt, staring up at the night skies looking wistful and angelic. He'd never asked her what she'd been doing, but guessed she'd been wishing on a star. That was the real Corinne. A woman struggling with trials and dreams, yet through it all, believing in something pure and real.

He knocked on the door and waited.

"Can I help you?" said a woman's voice on the other side of the door.

"Sandee?"

"Yes?"

"My name's Leo. I'd like to talk with you."

There was a pause, then the door clicked open. She looked like Corinne, eerily so, but Leo also picked up on distinct differences. Like the flame-red hair. And Sandee had a "seen it all" look in her eyes, a savviness Corinne didn't have. Plus he detected a spicy, exotic perfume, the opposite of Corinne's signature rose scent. Damn, he missed that rose scent.

"Leo," Sandee said, her blue eyes meeting his gaze. "Corinne's not here."

He thought how her eyes were a pretty blue, almost gray, but not the rich, velvety gray of Corinne's. God, he never imagined what everything "gray" would come to mean for him. Or how much he might miss looking into her eyes. Sandee's steady blue ones were staring at him, waiting for him to say something. "I, uh, know Corinne's not here. I wanted to talk to you." He cleared his throat, more to cover his anguish than anything else.

"Come inside," Sandee said, motioning him with a tilt of her head.

Stepping into the living room brought back another rush of memories...hot, passionate ones. He pulled on the neck of his shirt—these intense memories were damn near suffocating him. "I can only stay a moment."

"Leo," Sandee said, facing him squarely. "I'm going to tell it to you straight." She took a deep breath. "Here's the deal. Corinne thinks you got us mixed up. That you don't really care for her, the real Corinne, but for the act she played being me. You know, the ring-card girl bit."

"That's ridiculous," he snapped.

"I feel the same way." She opened her hands—her fingernails an outrageous pink, Leo noted—as though she agreed, but could do nothing about it. "That girl's been through a lot. And my take is she's not sure what to believe in, except for one thing..."

Leo waited. "And that is?"

"Her baby." Sandee dropped her hands. "She didn't tell me *not* to tell you, but even if she had, I couldn't have hidden this from you. She just found out today that she's pregnant. You're the father."

He felt as though he were bolted to the floor, scared spitless, and at the same time, slapped with joy. He didn't need to be told he was the father, he *knew* he was. Corinne had told him her fiancé hadn't touched her in months, but he'd have known without that confession, too. When they'd made love, he'd occasionally caught a tentativeness in her eyes, felt a hesitancy in her embrace, and knew this woman had not only gone without intimacy, but gone without love for a long time.

"A baby," he said, relishing the word. A warm contentment spread through him...and slammed into a cold front. "And she doesn't tell me?" The greatest gift he could imagine—a *child*—and the mother hides it from him?

"There's more."

His stomach tightened. "She's going back to Tony?"

"No. She's...leaving."

"Leaving?" He flashed on her in that pink convertible. "Now?" He shouldn't have let her drive away...he should have followed her!

"Not this *moment*," Sandee answered. "She's just picking up something at the store. She's leaving in a couple of days."

Considering she left her life in Denver within *seconds*, he had no doubt she'd split Vegas in a matter of days. He paced, feeling cornered with these facts, these complicated, hot and cold emotions.

Sandee's husky voice interrupted his thoughts. "Did you ever tell her you loved her?"

He stopped. He'd thought it, but... He shook his head no.

"Men," she said under her breath. "You know, if you *feel* it, you can *say* it. But most of you guys think if you say 'I love you' somebody's gonna shackle you and throw you into prison." She huffed a breath. "Marriage prison, I mean."

He knew what she'd meant. He'd been so burned

after Elizabeth, he'd sworn off going that route again. He grimaced, recalling how he'd told Corinne he might love again, but never again sign papers. Combine that foot-in-the-mouth moment with his calling her the wrong name, and of course she'd steer clear of him. "Sometimes guys are stupid," he conceded. "Especially this one."

"Well, everyone deserves a second chance." Sandee glanced at her ring, then continued. "She's come into some money, which I'm hoping she'll use to start over somewhere that'll be good for the baby. She doesn't know where yet, but somewhere other than Vegas or Denver."

"That leaves a lot of other places," he said darkly.

"If I knew where, I'd tell you. Trust me, after what Hank and I have been through, truth is a priority."

"Yes, Hank certainly pulled his act together." When he saw the question in Sandee's eyes, Leo explained, "I'm a detective. Heard the whole story at the precinct."

"So *you're* the detective." Sandee blinked. "Corinne told me about you, but I didn't know you were *also* Leo." She folded her arms. "So, you must know about that old guy, Willy, who did the bump and run on Tony?"

This took Leo a moment to digest. "Maybe you should be a detective, too. No, this is news to me."

"Oh." Sandee hesitated. "Well, I'm telling you so you'll know where the money came from—or where *I* think it came from. Because even if that money has questionable roots, there's nobody to legitimately return it to. And it'd be put to far better use for Corinne and the baby than wasted somewhere else." She glanced at a carton of cigarettes on the coffee table, heaved a sigh, then returned her gaze to Leo. "Here's the story. As you know, Hank—my fiancé—made amends with Willy, who pleaded with the judge to not send Hank to jail."

"Yes, I'm aware Hank got off easy." He was listening because this somehow affected Corinne, although, he was still in shock...a *baby*...it took every spare ounce of his concentration to absorb Sandee's words.

"A thousand hours community service is not only getting off easy, it's Lady Luck giving Hank a second chance." Sandee gave a grateful smile. "Fast forward," she went on. "Over a beer one night, Hank told Willy about my cousin and her no-good fiancé Tony..."

"Let me guess," Leo finished for her. "Willy, enraged that a good woman had been treated badly, over a Ferrari to boot, decided to pull his own bump and run."

Sandee nodded. "Yep. Rear-ended Tony's Ferrari, then stole it when Tony got out to exchange insurance information. That's what Hank thinks, and he swears *he* didn't do it, so I think it's Willy, too."

"And even though Willy and Hank are now best buds, Willy knows better than to confess to Hank that he'd pulled a copycat bump and run himself." Leo quickly assimilated the facts. A car like that, sold on the black market, would get a nice chunk of change. The money could never be traced. "Looks like Willy pulled a Robin Hood. Taking from the rich and giving to the poor." Taking from Tony and giving back to Corinne.

"I tried to convince her to keep it. Told her she owes it to her baby—"

"It's my baby, too." Leo dragged his hand through his hair. "Sorry, it's just I never got a chance to explain things to her." Never quite got it himself until just now. That he wanted love, still wanted a marriage, a real one, and...children. He wanted Corinne, not the woman she pretended to be, but the one in his arms...the one in the grocery aisle. *She* gave him reason to dream of a better life.

And now she was leaving?

He understood. He couldn't stay in this town, either. Not two more years or even two more days. Not without Corinne.

A few weeks ago, he'd learned life wasn't black or white. Thanks to Corinne, he'd chanced stepping into the middle ground, the gray, and accepting the contradictions within himself and others. But not being black and white, he now realized, was also a curse. Because at this moment he knew that no matter where he went, a shadow of Corinne—like a slice of gray— would always haunt him.

"I'm not walking away from the woman I love and my baby," he growled, "without fighting for them both."

JUGGLING A GROCERY BAG, Corinne opened the door to Sandee's apartment. "Guess what?" she called out to her cousin, "they had a special on eggplant, so I figured I'd teach you how to cook parmigiana, too!" She shut the door behind her with her foot, looked up and froze.

"Leo," she whispered. She stared wordlessly at

him, her heart pounding. She hadn't seen him in weeks. He looked edgier, more tired. *Over work...or over me?*

He stepped forward, took the bag, and set it on the coffee table. Turning back to her, he searched her face, his green eyes sparking fire. "You have a hell of a lot of nerve."

He knows. How much, Corinne wasn't sure. She felt a rush of anger at Sandee, which was quickly replaced by a fury all Corinne's own. How many times had Tony acted possessive, demanded answers, chided her for some decision she'd made? Well, the old Corinne took that behavior from a man, but not the new. She crossed her arms under her chest. "Finally, yes. I've got nerve to spare, Leo, and this is none of your business."

Leo glowered. "Maybe your decision to *leave* isn't my business, but the baby is."

So Sandee had spilled everything. Corinne started to say something, but after her bravado opening, she suddenly couldn't find the breath to speak. *The baby. He wants the baby.* But it was a package deal. He had to want Corinne, too...and the man wanted someone she'd pretended to be. "I can take care of myself and my baby," she whispered, not addressing his comment directly.

"So I've heard." He paced, like a caged animal, then stopped. His eyes glistened with pain, as though he were warring against himself. The way he looked reminded her of that night when their passion had exploded, right in this same room. Just like then, Leo leaned forward, his body tensed, like an animal ready to pounce. And just like that night, the air felt charged, thick with unspoken need....

Instinctively, she opened her arms....

With a guttural moan, he closed the space between them, crowding her against him. Shoving his face close, he murmured, "Damn it, Corinne, I love you." He kissed her roughly, all probing tongue and fierce need.

Fire spread through her. She clutched at his back, tugging him closer, wanting him, desiring him...

And who did he desire? Stiff-armed, she pushed him away. "You want the baby, but not me," she said hoarsely.

"Bull—"

She cut him off. "You don't even know me, Leo!" When he started to deny it, she interrupted again. "I've already done this. Committed myself to a man because my head was in the clouds, but he didn't truly love me. He loved the idea of having a wife and two-point-five kids—someday—but he didn't love *me*."

His jaw tightened. "Just because I slipped and called you Sandee—"

"It's more than that. It's my wearing bare-all clothes, prancing around in killer heels, wearing gobs of makeup, acting like a sexy ring-card girl...I'm not that person." When he started to speak again, she laid a finger gently against his lips. "Please, you shouldn't defend yourself. Don't tell me what I want to hear, what you think you believe. We'd be making a big mistake to start a life together. We've both crashed and burned before. Let's not do it again."

He paused, his face contorted with pain. "Don't do this, Corinne. Don't go."

"I have to." Before she gave in to the same old mistake the same old Corinne would have made.

He grimaced. She saw pain she couldn't quite believe. "You're wrong."

"I'm not."

"I'm in love with you, Corinne."

"You're not." Her eyes stung. How long could she stay strong, stay true to her resolve? "I'm leaving. You won't change my mind."

"Give me a chance."

"I can't, Leo. I won't settle again for a man who doesn't love me." She could only whisper now. "Not even my baby's father."

A steely look came into his eyes. He headed toward the front door, paused, then opened it. A light breeze wafted in, carrying a hint of roses. Over his shoulder, Leo said quietly, "You're a stronger woman, Corinne, than the one who ran away from Denver. Are you too strong now? Too hardened to take my love?"

"Leo—"

"Because I'm offering it all to you, everything you ever dreamed of. A home filled with children, made by two people who love each other more than anything else on this crazy planet..."

And in that instant when she had the chance to respond, her old fears stopped her from speaking. Then the door shut, its sharp click ending the conversation.

"I WANT MERLOT."

"You want, you want..." Leo picked up Mel's cage and looked through its metal bars at his parrot. "What you better want is to take a trip, 'cause that's what's next in the life of Mel, VD, and Leo." Leo looked around his living room, whose sole remaining object was the old leather chair, which he'd bequeathed to Dom. "You and I spent a lot of time here, buddy. A lot of Merlot under the bridge."

"I want Merlot."

"That's what you think." Leo carried the cage to the front door, which was wide open. Morning sunshine, hot and bright, spilled its buttery light across the hard-wood floor. "After that little pecking wine-opener trick, I tossed the rest of the bottles. You're on the wagon, Mel."

Leo walked outside, breathing in the scents of baked earth and jasmine. Vegas had always been his home, but even wolves left their territories. It was time for Leo to leave his. As he'd told Dom yesterday, he didn't want to put in two more years on the force...he wanted to take his chances now. If he'd learned any-thing this last year, it was that life is short. Rather than prowl the seamy side of Vegas for the next two years, he could do something he liked, hell maybe loved, while supporting his child—he'd send money to San-dee every month, with instructions to forward it to Corinne—and he'd save money for his small ranch. Maybe he'd get a gig as a P.I., maybe something else. Didn't matter.

He told Dom all that, but didn't add that not a whole lot mattered after losing Corinne.

Leo headed to the Bullet, its silver shell sparkling in the sunshine. He'd finished loading the trailer this morning. Well, packing up a TV, several boxes of books and six TV trays wasn't exactly "loading," but it was everything in the world he owned. And one thing he'd purchased last night, after leaving Sandee's apartment, which he wanted to drop off on his way out of town.

As he rounded the front end of the trailer, he heard a distinct tap tap tap.

Leo looked down at the cage. "What're you doing, Mel?"

Mel cocked his green-feathered head. *Squawk!*

Tap tap tap.

Mel wasn't pecking anything, so the sound had to be coming from somewhere else. Leo looked up. Propped in the window of the Airstream was one of those large white index cards, on which was neatly penned "Take me."

Take me?

He scanned the area, but all he saw was the empty street, the yard of small white rocks. Nobody was around.

He looked back at the sign. *Take me.* The words Corinne had said that night, the first night they made love. And again, that morning in the bedroom. He'd always remember her voice—soft, urgent. And the way her eyes darkened with desire.

From behind the sign, a small hand appeared. It tapped on the glass.

His heart banged against his chest. Just a few feet away, the trailer door was open. But the way it angled, it effectively blocked his view inside. With great effort, he picked up his feet and walked the few steps to see inside. Emotions imploding within him, he looked into the darkened cabin.

"Corinne." It was all he could say.

She stood just inside the trailer. Because its floor was a few feet off the ground, it gave him the crazy impression she was on a pedestal. She wore a loose, cream-colored shift dotted with tiny red and blue flowers. Her hair was pulled back from her face, accentuating those big, gray eyes. They looked luminous, like two shadowed pools hiding secret lights. What were those secrets? Why was she here?

Corinne stared at Leo, as though seeing him for the first time. He wore a simple white T-shirt and khaki shorts. It matched the rest of his pared-down look. His unruly hair had been trimmed. His beard, shaved. It was as though he'd stripped his life of anything extraneous.

He'd changed, and yet that look in his eyes she'd seen before. An aching tenderness that filled her with a soul-deep yearning. "Take me," she whispered, her voice catching. "Take me with you."

He set down the cage. "Where do you want to go Corinne? To some city where I can drop you off so you can start your life over?"

"I don't want to go anywhere like that." Corinne paused, committed to her course now, here in his Silver Bullet, but suddenly very afraid she might have hurt him so much that he would turn her away this time. She licked her lips. Damn, this was hard, letting this bullheaded man know what she wanted. Obviously the sign wasn't enough, so she'd have to spell it out. "I want you to take me wherever you're going." When he didn't respond, she felt as though a fist was squeezing her heart. Maybe she'd overreacted, avoiding him, then not telling him right away about the baby. After what he'd been through with Elizabeth, maybe Leo viewed Corinne as another game player.

Maybe he didn't want her to leave with him.

She hesitated, fighting a surge of emotions that threatened to undermine her resolve. No, she'd come too far to give up. If she'd risked starting her life over once, she could damn well do it again. At the MGM Grand, she'd seen gamblers stake everything they had on one play. Well, that's what she'd do now.

"I had to be strong, Leo, but...I'm not too strong to accept your love. I want to live the rest of my life with you..." Her insides fluttered madly. She laid it out, said what she wanted, so why didn't he say something?

Finally he did. "Do you believe I love you, Corinne? *You*. Not who you pretended to be?"

She nodded, touching the gold pendant. "I worried that you hadn't fallen for me, but for—"

"A hot bikini babe?" He laughed a little ruefully. "I'm a man, but I have a brain cell or two. You gave quite a show, but what I saw is a whole lot more than the wrapping." He stepped closer to the trailer and eyed the pendant. "Is that new?"

"No. It's my mother's...the only thing from my old life that I still have."

He shook his head. "You still have your truest self, the Corinne I fell in love with." He stared at her for a long moment. "I'll take you for a joyride, Corinne," he said solemnly, "but on one condition."

Her pulse raced. "Yes?"

"That it lasts a lifetime. I'll only take you as my wife."

"Oh-h-h, yes," she whispered, luxuriating in a sweet rush of emotions. "Can I tell you something?"

He raised his eyebrows in surprise. "About time," he teased.

She reached into her shift pocket, pulled out an envelope and opened it, revealing its emptiness. "I know Sandee told you about the money, which I gave back to the police. Said I didn't know where it came from, which is true."

Leo grinned. That lopsided grin that turned her insides liquid. "Well, I have something to show you, too." He reached inside the trailer, into a paper bag next to the door, and she heard a vaguely familiar sound, then recognized the object in his hand.

"The baby rattle," she whispered, looking at the white rattle with Tweety Bird on it. The rattle she'd played with in the supermarket that night. "How'd you—?" She smiled, then laughed. "You were following me when I was in that baby aisle!"

Squawk. "I want baby!"

"Mel," Leo said, looking down at the cage, "I couldn't have said it better myself." He looked back at her, his green eyes sparkling like sunlight on the sea. "Honey, I want you, I want this baby...and the next baby, and the next..." He moved closer and opened his arms. "Come home, Corinne."

And she fell into his arms, embracing everything she'd ever dreamed of.

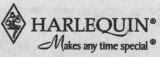

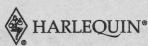

This Mother's Day Give Your Mom A Royal Treat

Win a fabulous one-week vacation in Puerto Rico for you and your mother at the luxurious Inter-Continental San Juan Resort & Casino. The prize includes round trip airfare for two, breakfast daily and a mother and daughter day of beauty at the beachfront hotel's spa.

INTER·CONTINENTAL
San Juan
RESORT & CASINO

Here's all you have to do:

Tell us in 100 words or less how your mother helped with the romance in your life. It may be a story about your engagement, wedding or those boyfriends when you were a teenager or any other romantic advice from your mother. The entry will be judged based on its originality, emotionally compelling nature and sincerity. See official rules on following page.

Send your entry to:

Mother's Day Contest

In Canada
P.O. Box 637
Fort Erie, Ontario
L2A 5X3

In U.S.A.
P.O. Box 9076
3010 Walden Ave.
Buffalo, NY
14269-9076

Or enter online at www.eHarlequin.com

HARLEQUIN MOTHER'S DAY CONTEST 2216
OFFICIAL RULES
NO PURCHASE NECESSARY TO ENTER

Two ways to enter:

• **Via The Internet:** Log on to the Harlequin romance website (www.eHarlequin.com) anytime beginning 12:01 a.m. E.S.T., January 1, 2002 through 11:59 p.m. E.S.T., April 1, 2002 and follow the directions displayed on-line to enter your name, address (including zip code), e-mail address and in 100 words or fewer, describe how your mother helped with the romance in your life.

• **Via Mail:** Handprint (or type) on an 8 1/2" x 11" plain piece of paper, your name, address (including zip code) and e-mail address (if you have one), and in 100 words or fewer, describe how your mother helped with the romance in your life. Mail your entry via first-class mail to: Harlequin Mother's Day Contest 2216, (in the U.S.) P.O. Box 9076, Buffalo, NY 14269-9076; (in Canada) P.O. Box 637, Fort Erie, Ontario, Canada L2A 5X3.

For eligibility, entries must be submitted either through a completed Internet transmission or postmarked no later than 11:59 p.m. E.S.T., April 1, 2002 (mail-in entries must be received by April 9, 2002). Limit one entry per person, household address and e-mail address. On-line and/or mailed entries received from persons residing in geographic areas in which entry is not permissible will be disqualified.

Entries will be judged by a panel of judges, consisting of members of the Harlequin editorial, marketing and public relations staff using the following criteria:
• Originality - 50%
• Emotional Appeal - 25%
• Sincerity - 25%

In the event of a tie, duplicate prizes will be awarded. Decisions of the judges are final.

Prize: A 6-night/7-day stay for two at the Inter-Continental San Juan Resort & Casino, including round-trip coach air transportation from gateway airport nearest winner's home (approximate retail value: $4,000). Prize includes breakfast daily and a mother and daughter day of beauty at the beachfront hotel's spa. Prize consists of only those items listed as part of the prize. Prize is valued in U.S. currency.

All entries become the property of Torstar Corp. and will not be returned. No responsibility is assumed for lost, late, illegible, incomplete, inaccurate, non-delivered or misdirected mail or misdirected e-mail, for technical, hardware or software failures of any kind, lost or unavailable network connections, or failed, incomplete, garbled or delayed computer transmission or any human error which may occur in the receipt or processing of the entries in this Contest.

Contest open only to residents of the U.S. (except Colorado) and Canada, who are 18 years of age or older and is void wherever prohibited by law; all applicable laws and regulations apply. Any litigation within the Province of Quebec respecting the conduct or organization of a publicity contest may be submitted to the Régie des alcools, des courses et des jeux for a ruling. Any litigation respecting the awarding of a prize may be submitted to the Régie des alcools, des courses et des jeux only for the purpose of helping the parties reach a settlement. Employees and immediate family members of Torstar Corp. and D.L. Blair, Inc., their affiliates, subsidiaries and all other agencies, entities and persons connected with the use, marketing or conduct of this Contest are not eligible to enter. Taxes on prize are the sole responsibility of winner. Acceptance of any prize offered constitutes permission to use winner's name, photograph or other likeness for the purposes of advertising, trade and promotion on behalf of Torstar Corp., its affiliates and subsidiaries without further compensation to the winner, unless prohibited by law.

Winner will be determined no later than April 15, 2002 and be notified by mail. Winner will be required to sign and return an Affidavit of Eligibility form within 15 days after winner notification. Non-compliance within that time period may result in disqualification and an alternate winner may be selected. Winner of trip must execute a Release of Liability prior to ticketing and must possess required travel documents (e.g. Passport, photo ID) where applicable. Travel must be completed within 12 months of selection and is subject to traveling companion completing and returning a Release of Liability prior to travel; and hotel and flight accommodations availability. Certain restrictions and blackout dates may apply. No substitution of prize permitted by winner. Torstar Corp. and/or D.L. Blair, Inc., their parents, affiliates, and subsidiaries are not responsible for errors in printing or electronic presentation of Contest, or entries. In the event of printing or other errors which may result in unintended prize values or duplication of prizes, all affected entries shall be null and void. If for any reason the Internet portion of the Contest is not capable of running as planned, including infection by computer virus, bugs, tampering, unauthorized intervention, fraud, technical failures, or any other causes beyond the control of Torstar Corp. which corrupt or affect the administration, secrecy, fairness, integrity or proper conduct of the Contest, Torstar Corp. reserves the right, at its sole discretion, to disqualify any individual who tampers with the entry process and to cancel, terminate, modify or suspend the Contest or the Internet portion thereof. In the event the Internet portion must be terminated a notice will be posted on the website and all entries received prior to termination will be judged in accordance with these rules. In the event of a dispute regarding an on-line entry, the entry will be deemed submitted by the authorized holder of the e-mail account submitted at the time of entry. Authorized account holder is defined as the natural person who is assigned to an e-mail address by an Internet access provider, on-line service provider or other organization that is responsible for arranging e-mail address for the domain associated with the submitted e-mail address. Torstar Corp. and/or D.L. Blair Inc. assumes no responsibility for any computer injury or damage related to or resulting from accessing and/or downloading any sweepstakes material. Rules are subject to any requirements/limitations imposed by the FCC. **Purchase or acceptance of a product offer does not improve your chances of winning.**

For winner's name (available after May 1, 2002), send a self-addressed, stamped envelope to: Harlequin Mother's Day Contest Winners 2216, P.O. Box 4200 Blair, NE 68009-4200 or you may access the www.eHarlequin.com Web site through June 3, 2002.

Contest sponsored by Torstar Corp., P.O. Box 9042, Buffalo, NY 14269-9042.

If you enjoyed what you just read,
then we've got an offer you can't resist!

Take 2 bestselling love stories FREE!

Plus get a FREE surprise gift!